"From the way you look at her...I thought the baby might be yours," Arthur said.

"I've only known her a couple of days. And she's *only* my consultant. That's all."

"With that look I saw in your eyes, Beau, I think you've known her a lifetime. Or wanted to know her." He grinned.

Beau snapped on a glove. "Moving on," he said to Arthur, his mind totally on Deanna.

He'd thought she was reserved, and after discovering she was pregnant now he knew why. Still, she didn't seem happy enough. Especially for someone who'd made the choice to bring a baby into the world on her own. It was a tough decision, but an exciting one. In Deanna, though, he saw confusion where he should have been seeing joy. There was something else, he decided. But he couldn't imagine what. More than that, he couldn't imagine why he cared. He did, though. He cared and he didn't want to explore the reason why. In fact he didn't even want to think that there might *be* a reason.

Dear Reader

A few years ago I met an amazing woman—Nona—who travelled by horse through the mountain regions of the eastern United States. What fascinated me about her was not so much that she spent day after day on the trail, in the woods, in the mountains, and in areas so isolated the world had forgotten them—I was fascinated by the fact that she was a doctor who packed her medicine into her saddle bags and took it to the people who lived in those areas. People who wouldn't have it otherwise.

At the time I guess I didn't even know such areas existed in the United States, much less that the people from those places didn't have access to the same things I had. But Nona was diligent in what she referred to as her 'calling', and she took her skills and knowledge to people who didn't take for granted the conveniences of life most of us are accustomed to having.

I like writing about people who, like Nona, have a similar calling. People who don't practise 'convenient' medicine. That's why you see this recurring theme in so many of my books. There are dedicated, quiet people in this world who serve without accolade. I've met them in my travels, been befriended by them, seen them work under conditions I can't even begin to describe. They do have a calling—a higher calling, I believe. And it's because of them I bring you the story of Deanna and Beau, who wrestle with the life they had in New York and the one they'll face together in a community one hundred miles from nowhere.

As always, wishing you health and happiness

Dianne

P.S. Check me out on Facebook at:
www.facebook.com/DianneDrakeAuthor

P.S. YOU'RE A DADDY!

BY
DIANNE DRAKE

First published in Great Britain 2013
by Mills & Boon, an imprint of Harlequin (UK) Limited.
Harlequin (UK) Limited, Eton House, 18-24 Paradise Road,
Richmond, Surrey TW9 1SR

© Dianne Despain 2013

ISBN: 978 0 263 23362 9

Harlequin (UK) policy is to use papers that are natural, renewable
and recyclable products and made from wood grown in sustainable
forests. The logging and manufacturing process conform to the
legal environmental regulations of the country of origin.

Printed and bound in Great Britain
by CPI Antony Rowe, Chippenham, Wiltshire

Now that her children have left home, **Dianne Drake** is finally finding the time to do some of the things she adores—gardening, cooking, reading, shopping for antiques. Her absolute passion in life, however, is adopting abandoned and abused animals. Right now Dianne and her husband Joel have a little menagerie of three dogs and two cats, but that's always subject to change. A former symphony orchestra member, Dianne now attends the symphony as a spectator several times a month and, when time permits, takes in an occasional football, basketball or hockey game.

To Doc Nona, with all my admiration.

CHAPTER ONE

ONE SIGH SAID it all, and for Deanna Lambert that sigh filled an entire story—past, present and future. She stared at her face in the mirror for a full minute, unsure what the face staring back was telling her. Do it? Don't do it? Keep your fingers crossed and hope for the best?

"You're no help," she groused at her image, then pulled up her red tank top and finally assembled the courage to look at her belly yet again. She brushed away another tear. Ups and downs now. That's what her life was about, ups and downs. "I wish I knew what to do. Wish somebody would just say, Deanna, do this." But situations like hers didn't come with a set of instructions. Only regret. More regret than she knew what to do with. And pain. Dear God, the pain nearly crippled her.

Assessing her belly, Deanna's new daily routine, she splayed her fingers over the warm flesh, willing herself to feel the child just beneath her fingertips. It was silly of her, of course, but this baby was her only connection to Emily, and she wanted desperately to hold onto that connection, feel that connection the way she used to. Count on it.

She couldn't, though. Not any more. But this baby…it was different. A hope she wasn't ready to accept. Permission to move on. A blessing ready to be claimed.

Another tear trickled down her cheek and she swatted at it with the back of her hand.

"Part of me wants to go and find him. He's your daddy." At least, biologically he was. "And maybe he would want to know about you." But the truth was, men who made sperm donations didn't want to know. It was an anonymous gesture, often for the money and sometimes out of generosity. Or ego. So which was it for Braxton Alexander? she wondered. The unbearable weight of not knowing was dragging her down. The unbearable weight of carrying her cousin's baby—a baby who would never see his or her mother—was dragging her down ever deeper.

"Resolve it immediately," Dr. Brewster, her obstetrician, had warned her. "Your blood pressure is borderline high, you're not getting enough sleep, you've lost three pounds. Regardless of whose baby you're carrying, you're that baby's lifeline. You've got to take better care of yourself. So figure out what you need to do, and do it."

Kindly old doctor. And he was right. She had to figure out what to do, and do it. "But darn," she murmured, as she backed away from the mirror and pulled down her top, "why couldn't somebody just tell me what it is I should do?"

She was in this alone. Carrying a mistaken baby—her cousin's child who, beyond a shadow of a doubt, was not the progeny of her cousin's husband. However a mistake like that could be made in this age of technological wizardry. *Oops, wrong sperm, Mrs. Braxton. We're terribly sorry.*

A mistake that had cost Emily her life, as it had turned out.

"It would have been good," she said to the baby. "Even if Alex didn't want you after he found out, Emily would have been the best mother anyone could have because she wanted you so badly." Even after three miscarriages and a stillbirth Emily had never lost hope. "And I would have helped you raise her." Deanna ran her hand over her red tank top to smooth the wrinkles but more to acknowledge the love she felt every time she touched her belly.

And she did love this child. She didn't feel equal to the task of motherhood, and hadn't ever even thought of herself in those terms, to be honest. But that didn't negate the feelings she had for Emily's baby. And those only grew stronger every day. Along with the irrational guilt. Survivor's guilt, she'd been told. "So, the question remains, should I tell your father about you, or let him exist as the anonymous donor he was?"

Stupid question. Anonymous donors wanted anonymity, presumably. But something was pulling her in a direction she knew she should resist. "OK, so maybe we could go there and simply watch him for a while, see what kind of man he is. What kind of genes you'll be getting from him. No harm in that, is there?"

No harm except the emotional one that kept her hanging onto something she didn't understand. Dr. Brewster was right. She had to resolve this. But by going all the way to Tennessee? Specifically, Sugar Creek? That's where the investigator she'd hired said he was living now. One law firm, a private investigator and some pretty formidable legal maneuvering had gained her a little information, more than most women had when they made their selections from the information inside the catalogs, and that should have been enough. But it wasn't.

And maybe that's because she really did want to know, or simply because hanging onto a man she should never, under any circumstances, meet meant putting off the inevitable—facing what happened next.

All she wanted to do was see him. Nothing else. And

wasn't it her right to know more about the father of the baby she carried? OK, so maybe it wasn't. But she was... curious. What, specifically, she wanted to know about him, she had no clue.

She did want to stop hurting, though, and maybe that's what this near obsession was about. Losing his cousin, her best friend, had turned into a pain she didn't know how anybody could endure, and she was looking for anything to make it stop. Maybe that's what finding Dr. Braxton Alexander was about, at least in part. Something to keep her occupied until something else made sense.

"So, we go to Sugar Creek," she said to the baby, looking at the already packed bags by her front door. They'd been packed for days, and she'd gone this far several times before. Then stopped. But today was different. She could feel it in her resolve, in her heart and, yes, in her belly. Today she would carry those bags to the car, climb in and head south. All the way to Tennessee.

"But before we leave, I need to stop by the cemetery and tell Emily what we're going to do," she told the baby. "Emily," she whispered, as tears started welling again. "I really don't know what I'm doing, and I'm so scared..."

"Welcome to Sugar Creek, Tennessee," Deanna said on an ambivalent sigh. This was it. She'd done it. Well, part of it. She'd managed to get herself here. As far as the next part went, she had options and she wasn't ready to decide which one to choose. So for now she was here to work. At least, that's what she'd tell people. Reports to do, financial donor sources to track down, people to hire who would implement her programs. Her temporary lease here was for a month and she'd brought enough work with her to keep her busy for three, so the part about coming here to work wasn't a lie. Nurse researcher with plenty to do.

Now, stepping out of her car and raising her binoculars to look down the south face of the mountain at the lay of the little town, she noted how the quaint buildings stretched pleasantly up and down Sugar Creek Highway. There was an outcropping of foothills and more green trees than she'd ever seen in any one place in her life jutting out prominently in any direction she looked other than the main part of town itself.

"It's very pretty. And it's got a grocery store, café, general merchandise store, and beauty shop. I think we'll have a nice month here." With or without tracking down Braxton Alexander.

Even though she'd never lived in one, Deanna loved small towns, loved the whole countrified experience. As a nurse researcher, she'd devoted her entire career to finding ways to make healthcare better in areas where it wasn't easily accessed. Places like Sugar Creek, which sat in a beautiful, secluded valley a hundred miles from anywhere. It wasn't the beauty of such places that caught her attention when she took on new assignments but the seclusion, because her job was to bridge the medical gaps.

"But this town is one of the lucky ones," she said. "It has a doctor. Your daddy." Your daddy... Odd how that was so easy to say. "Judging from what I read about him, he's very good." And she'd read everything she could find. A few articles he'd written about general surgery, some accounts of awards he'd received. Nothing about why he'd given up a lucrative New York City surgery to isolate himself here. As a GP, no less.

Midday carried with it a cool June breeze, and a chill washed over Deanna as she lowered her binoculars and, once again, thought about what she was doing here. Chasing Braxton Alexander. This wasn't just a small change of direction for her. It was a total life-changer. She was having this man's baby—a baby she'd never planned on having—and sitting on a mountaintop hoping to catch a glimpse of him somewhere.

How much more perverse did life get than that? She tilted her face to the sky and, for the first time in weeks, actually felt a little bit of relaxation slide down over her.

"I'm pretty sure I'm glad we came here, but I suppose there's a lot still to be determined." She liked talking to the baby, particularly here. Possibly because she was so close to the daddy. Or maybe because she'd put physical distance between herself and everything that reminded her of Emily.

"Now we're going to have to figure out what we're going to do next...*for real*." She laid her hand on her belly. "So, here are our options. We can watch and keep quiet. Try finding a way to meet him. Or we can always play it by ear. See what happens. Hope for the best."

However it worked out, she had a whole month ahead of her to find the answer and act on it. Or not.

"She's making eyes at you, boss." Joey Santiago led the chestnut mare into the stall then took off her lead before he stepped out and latched the door behind him. Brushing his hands together to shake off the dust, he said, "They all do it. Big brown eyes, so many expectations. You've let them have their way with you once too often, and now you pay for it every time you come in here."

"Not pay for it, Joey. Enjoy it." Beau leaned over the Dutch door of the stall and gave the mare a couple of lumps of sugar, like he always did. It's what he'd done as a child every time he'd spent a few days or a few months here with his grandfather, and he'd continued doing it after he'd moved in for good when he'd been a teenager.

"And they love you for it."

"Horses don't love," Beau protested. "They merely get used to certain things." The way he had, growing up. "Come to expect them. Recognize them when they're being offered."

"You're wrong there, Beau. They love, just like we do. You can see it in their eyes."

Joey had been here for as long as Beau could remember, doing odd jobs, gardening, taking care of the few horses his grandfather always kept, and taking care of Beau's grandfather after his stroke. He was also part of the two-man team who had raised him when his dad had gone off on benders and wherever else it was the old man had gone to avoid life, responsibility and, most of all, fatherhood.

"Some of us don't love, though," Beau countered, still cringing over his marriage fiasco nearly two years later.

"You loved," Joey countered. "Just not wisely. But with a horse you don't have to worry about duplicitous intentions. A carrot and a few kind words will get you unconditional love for ever. And even if you don't yet have a taste for falling in love again, that's going to change. Just in your own time."

"Or in no time," Beau quipped, preferring not to think about Nancy. Two years later, he still did, though. It was inevitable, he supposed, because of the way she'd changed his life. But all this love talk made him nervous. He wanted to climb up on one of these horses and ride so hard it knocked the memories right out of him.

Joey, a stocky man with thick black hair, shook his head as he peeked over the half-door in the next stall at Nell, who was ready to give birth any time. "I watched you at the races last spring, in Kentucky. Watched you get so excited when Donder almost won the Derby. I saw love in your eyes for that horse, Beau. I know you're not dead in your emotions like you think you are. Just holding it back."

"Emotionally dead is easier."

"Or safer. But that's going to change. Mark my words, when the time's right to move on, nothing's going to hold you back."

"I've been ready to move on for two years." And everything was holding him back.

"And yet you haven't," Joey quipped. "Strange how that works, isn't it?"

Joey was right, of course. But Beau didn't have to admit that out loud because, in ways he didn't want to deal with, he was just fine being held back. It kept him away from the possibility that what he'd gone through once could happen again. Admitting you'd been so blind and, on top of that, so insanely stupid on so many levels... No, there would be no repeat acts for him, and the only way to guarantee that was to keep his distance. Big distance.

"What's strange is standing here talking to you about my love life when I've got fences to mend out on the back forty." Barring emergencies, no more patients for the day and no house calls for the evening. With any luck he'd be so worn out by nightfall that, for once, a good night's sleep—out there—would come easily. Then he'd get an early jump on it in the morning and be back here by noon to open the clinic. But he had to quit talking first. And quit moping as well.

"So which one you running away from? Thinking about that whole mess you had with your wife, or the problems you've got going with Brax?"

Leave it to Joey to turn one emotional train wreck into two. He loved the man, knew he only wanted to help. But, damn, not this way. "I've got no problems with the old man," Beau snapped. "Just a difference of medical opinion." Big difference of opinion.

Joey chuckled. "Your way, his way. Two stubborn men

who don't want to budge. Glad the extent of my medical knowledge doesn't go beyond applying a bandage and some good, old-fashioned horse medicine."

True, they were alike in a few ways. Stubbornness for stubbornness, maybe they did match up, but only a little bit. "OK, so maybe we have *some* similarities. But the old man thinks he can practice medicine again, and I know he can't. It's time for him to retire."

"Two peas in a pod. Actually, let's make that two peas in separate pods since you're not seeing eye to eye on pretty much anything right now."

It bothered Beau more than he let on. He liked being here, on Brax's land, close to nature, in a place where no one could touch him. It let him remember the best times of his life when he and his grandfather would go out to mend fences together then stay over for a camp-out.

He missed those uncomplicated days. Missed his once uncomplicated life. But the complications came from so many directions now—some of his doing, some from Brax's physical condition. Too many bitter pills to swallow.

"That's why I'm going out for the night. Brax and I need some space. There's too much conflict going on in the house and it's not good for him."

"Not good for you either."

"But I'm not trying to recover from a stroke."

"A little space might be good. I'll give you that. But what if Nell decides that tonight's her night? Or there's a medical emergency?"

"Call me." He patted the pocket of his chambray shirt, where his cellphone was tucked away. "Or come get me in the helicopter." Yes, Brax had a helicopter. A necessity in these spread-out parts for a GP who still made house calls. "And I'm fine to be out there by myself, brooding about my life and all the things I can't fix, so quit worrying about me, OK?" Actually, he was looking forward to going up to his spot to contemplate his past, present, even his future. Because right now it was one big blur, and he wasn't sure about any of it.

"You up on the ridge all alone, your grandfather holed up in his study all alone... Like I said, different pods, same peas."

Beau chuckled, and patted Joey on the back. "Leave me the hell alone, will you? The last thing I need is all that perception hanging around me, making too much sense." The truth was, he was still in a wallowing mood, and he'd become damned good at it.

"You're not going to find a better view anywhere in Sugar Creek," Kelli Dawson said, as she pushed back the double doors and invited Deanna to step outside onto the porch to the see the view. Kelli was the rental agent, giving Deanna the grand tour of her home for the next month. "Hot tub in the left corner, porch swing in the right. And look at everything you can see from here."

It was breathtaking, Deanna did have to admit. And the photos Kelli had e-mailed didn't do this cabin justice. "But you're going to sell it?"

"I'm just the listing agent. My client wants to sell, but it's been on the market a year now and nobody's interested. Sugar Creek is a nice town, but it's small, too isolated. Our doctor here has to use a helicopter to make house calls."

Braxton Alexander was the doctor, but she needed to hear it acknowledged. "Your doctor is...?"

"Doc Brax. Wonderful man. Everybody loves him." That was encouraging. It was nice to know the baby's daddy was liked. "He's been an institution here for ever. Delivered most of the babies around here. Including me!"

No way...! According to the donor card, Braxton Alexander was thirty-six. Was she chasing after the wrong person? Wasting her time, not to mention her emotional investment, in the wrong place?

"And he's still delivering babies?"

"Not since his stroke. He recovered from it pretty well. Needs a cane sometimes to help him get around better. But I'd still let him be my doctor if he hadn't quit, because his mind's as sharp as ever. By the time my grandpa was Doc Brax's age, he was forgetful and he just seemed so withered up. But Doc Brax looks good for his age, and Joey, the man who runs Braxton Acres, says he'll be able to get rid of his cane any day now."

"How old is Doc Brax?"

"Seventy-five, I think. Could be seventy-six."

Not the baby's daddy, then, unless the sperm bank had got that wrong, too. "He's the only doctor in this area?"

"He was, until his grandson Braxton, known as Beau took over. Good doctor, but not friendly like his grandfather. People don't think he likes being back here... He used to be the town troublemaker when he was a kid. But he does what he's supposed to now, and he's as good as his grandfather, so the rest of it doesn't really matter." Her smile widened.

"Upstairs you'll find the game room and TV. Downstairs you'll find the laundry and a couple of extra bedrooms. And on this level...you've seen it all. The kitchen, the great room. Oh, and there's a whirlpool in the master suite."

"It's lovely," Deanna said absently, her mind still on the Braxton Alexander who'd fathered Emily's baby. Good doctor a plus, lacking in personality a minus. Troublemaker as a kid an even bigger minus! "I think everything will suit me just fine."

"You can call out for groceries, too. Number's by the

phone. If you want to hole up for the entire month and never leave, you can. So, what was it you said you were going to do? Write a book?"

Sugar Creek, where everybody knew everybody else's business. That could work to her advantage, or against it. One way or the other, she was going to have to be very careful here, because her business was nobody else's. "Something like that."

"Well, if you find yourself craving company, my office is on the main street. Stop by any time. We can have lunch or I can show you around. There's not much to do here so it's always nice to make new friends."

She liked Kelli. Maybe under other circumstances they might have been friends. But she wasn't here about friendship, wasn't here to have lunches or insert herself into the local culture. This trip was only about finding out what kind of man had fathered Emily's baby, and once her curiosity was satisfied, she'd leave. Hopefully she would return to the larger apartment her own real estate agent was scouting for her right now. Another of those life changes happening too fast.

After hastily unpacking and tossing a few articles of clothing on the bed rather than hanging them, Deanna fixed herself a pitcher of lemonade and headed out to the porch swing. This was her next month: sitting, watching, hoping to learn. So why not start it now?

"They say your daddy isn't too personable," she said, laying her hand protectively over her belly as she lowered herself into the swing. "But that doesn't really matter, does it? Not to either of us. I want you and love you, so it's going to be fine even if he is an old grump." Although somehow she'd wanted him to be pleasant, and she was a little disappointed by the prospect that he wasn't. "So what else are we going to discover?"

The truth was, now that she was here, she was scared about it, and feeling more alone than she ever had in her life. "But we'll get through it," she said. "I always do." A fact that scared her even more because, for the first time since she'd agreed to carry this baby, she realized she didn't want to do it alone. But alone was what she was.

So very alone. And nothing could fix that. "So now I'm going to cry," she said as the tears welled in her eyes. "Damn the hormones." And the loneliness.

CHAPTER TWO

IT UNVEILED ITSELF before her eyes, almost in slow motion. Even from her mountaintop perch she saw the beginning of it, two cars climbing up the modestly steep highway leading into town, one in the front, one bringing up the rear at a safe distance.

Nothing out of the ordinary except the deer that darted out in front of the first car then paused in the middle of the road to stare at its would-be attacker, and run safely off to the other side. All this while the first car swerved to avoid it then jammed on its brakes, sending it into a fish-tail that caused it to cut in and out, from lane to lane, over the center line, then whip back to the other side. Correcting and over-correcting to right itself.

That's when the full realization of what she was witnessing grabbed hold and propelled her off the swing and right up to the rail of the porch for a better look. And as that horrible realization sank in deeper, and the second car jammed on its brakes to avoid the veering of the first car, her hand crept to her pocket and her fingers wrapped around her cellphone as the second car braked too hard and skidded…and skidded…and skidded…

A sickening crunch of metal permeated the mountain air, one so hideous it caused a roost of black birds in a far-off tree to flee their sanctuary with great protest and screeching. Holding her breath, Deanna didn't divert her eyes from the road below as her fingers slid over the phone's smooth face. She glanced down just long enough to see the numbers to push, and pushed.

Then, as she looked back down the side of the mountain, the second car was flipping, side over side, repeatedly hitting the pavement. Its course to the edge of the road clear, the clutching in her heart turning to a stabbing pain. "Dear God," she murmured, as the emergency dispatcher came on.

"This is 911, what's your emergency?"

"No," Deanna cried in a strangled scream, hoping God or somebody would hear her and stop the second car's inevitable plummet over the side of the mountain.

"What's your emergency?" the dispatcher asked again, followed by, "Miss Lambert, are you all right? Please, can you hear me?"

Hearing her name snapped her back into the moment. "Yes, I'm here, and I'm watching a wreck in progress. Two cars..." She glanced left, to the semi heading down the mountain, its driver not yet able to see what was ahead. "And maybe a semi, if it doesn't get stopped in..." Her voice trailed off as she watched the second act unfold.

"Where, Miss Lambert?"

Again, hearing her name from the dispatcher jolted her. "It's a road I can see from my porch, but I don't know its name. I'm in my cabin..."

"Above the Clouds," the dispatcher supplied, then asked, "South porch?"

"Yes."

"Can you tell me, exactly, what kind of damage or injuries we might be looking at?"

Massive, devastating injuries, she thought. "Yes. One of the cars has just gone through the guardrail and over the edge. And the other..." She swallowed hard. "It hit the guardrail a few times and it's still trying to correct itself on the road... I think the truck coming from the other direction's going to hit it."

Whether or not the driver of the semi saw the impending disaster ahead, or simply assumed the car careening head first at him in his lane would move over, Deanna had no idea, but the excruciating squeal of the semi's brakes and the low wail of the truck's horn was what snapped her totally out of the surreal watching mode and into action.

"I know exactly where it is," the dispatcher said, "and I've sent out an alarm to the volunteer fire department. They'll be there as fast as they can."

How long would that be? In a study concerning rural emergency response times Deanna had conducted last year, she'd discovered that those waiting times could be fatally long—sometimes thirty minutes, up to an hour. And from what she'd just witnessed, there were people down below who needed help before that. "What about the local doctor?" she asked. "Can we call him?"

"He's out mending fences right now, but I'll give his grandpa a call and see what we can do to get him there. Kelli Dawson's my daughter, by the way. And I know this is probably not the best time to say this, but welcome to Sugar Creek, Miss Lambert."

She heard the cordial greeting, but it wasn't registering because... "Oh, my... No!" The semi didn't hit the oncoming car, as she'd thought it might, but in its attempt to do a hard brake, it jackknifed and turned over, sliding on its side along the road.

And the car swerved right into it, hit the back end of its trailer with full-on force, bringing both the truck and the car to a stop. "More casualties," she informed Kelli's mother. "Two cars and one semi now. Can't see how many people..." Wasn't sure she wanted to see how many people.

But after she'd clicked off from the dispatcher, curiosity got the better of her and she grabbed her binoculars, took a look. Nobody was moving. No one was trying to climb out of the carnage. No one was trying to climb up the side of the mountain from where they'd toppled off.

And there was no one there to help. That's what scared her the most. People down there needed help and she prayed they weren't past the point where help mattered.

Without a thought for anything else, Deanna grabbed her medical kit, one she carried out of habit more than necessity, and sprinted for her car. She backed it out and headed down the steep road, making sure not to speed lest she ended up like one of the cars below. At the turn-off to the highway, she slowed to let a minivan by, made a left-hand turn and headed for the crash site, hoping help would be there when she arrived.

But the minivan was the only car present, and the woman driving it was standing outside her vehicle, torn between running to look for victims and trying to subdue three small children in the rear of the van. Her cellphone was in her hand and she was physically standing in front of the van's door. Was she trying to block the view from her children? Deanna wondered about that as she pulled alongside the van, waved to the woman, then continued to drive into the heart of the scene.

It's what she would do, she realized. She would protect Emily's baby from seeing what she herself was about to confront. She absolutely understood that mothering priority. She wasn't sure she'd respond that way in a crisis out of a natural tendency but, looking at it from a purely practical point of view, there was no denying the minivan mom was doing what she had to do. Something Deanna hoped she would learn when she became a mom.

As Deanna brought her car to a stop, several hundred yards short of the crash site, her cellphone jingled before she had a chance to step out. "You're a nurse?" the deep voice practically shouted. He sounded winded.

"I am. And who are you?"

"Local doctor. Beau…"

She wasn't even going to ask how he knew who she was, that she was a nurse, her cellphone number… "Your ETA?"

"Five minutes, tops. But without supplies. You're on the site already?"

How did he know that? "Just got here. Don't know how many victims yet."

"OK, you go see what we've got and I'll keep the line open, Miss Lambert. And please start the assessments, establish the priority if you can, figure out what I need to do first, and I'll be there as fast as I can."

He knew her name, too. And trusted her to prioritize the scene? She hadn't done that in a while. Hadn't been in active practice for years. Maybe if she'd told him that, he wouldn't be so trusting of her.

Those were the thoughts that stayed with her for the next seconds as she grabbed her medical bag, switched her phone to her earpiece, and headed straight for the first car. "I'm not sure we're cut out for small-town life," she whispered to Emily's baby as she went straight to the driver's-side window of the car that had hit the semi, and looked in.

"In case you're listening, Doctor, I have a red sedan embedded in the back of the semi's trailer. Inside, three people. Male, mid-twenties, driver. Female passenger, approximately same age. Both unconscious. Airbags not deployed. No seat belts. From what I can see, both have had head contact with the windshield, profuse cranial bleeding both victims. Not seeing movement of any kind. And back seat..."

She bent, took a closer look, and was hit with a cold chill. "Child, age approximately three. No child seat. No seat belt. And..." she pulled open the car door and kneeled inside "...he's conscious."

"Stay with the child, Miss Lambert. Do you hear me? Stay with the child. I'm a minute away."

Not that she would have left this little boy. "Hello," she said, crawling all the way in. Instinctively, she reached over the front seat, took the driver's pulse. Found nothing. "My name is Deanna," she said to the toddler. He was curled up in a ball on the floor, looking at her with huge blue eyes that registered shock and terror and total confusion. "Can you tell me your name?"

Crawling across the seat until she was above the little boy, she leaned forward until she could get a good positioning on the female passenger's neck and, again, felt no pulse. "Can you tell me where you hurt?" Were his parents both dead? Admittedly, she wasn't in the best position to make assessments on the couple, so she wasn't making any assumptions.

"No pulses detected," she said to the vague voice on the phone. "Nothing affirmative, though. I'm not at a good angle to tell."

"But you're in the car?" he asked.

"Yes, with the child."

"Is the car safe? No fuel leaking, nothing that looks like it's going to ignite? Not close to the edge of the road?"

"Front end's a mangled mess, but I'm safe." She was pleased he actually sounded concerned.

"No chances, Miss Lambert. You keep yourself safe. Do you hear me?"

Yes, she heard him. "I have every intention of doing

just that, Doctor," she replied. To get Emily's baby safely into the world, she would take no risks.

"Is the child injured? Can you tell if he's hurt?"

"Can't tell yet. I'm trying to check, but it's cramped in here." Cramped, even without her baby bump. She wondered how, in months to come, she was going to maneuver *with* a baby bump. "We'll just have to wait and see how that works out," she said to Emily's baby.

"Yes, I suppose we will have to see how it works out. In the meantime, I'm coming up behind you, so hold tight."

Startled that she'd been caught talking to Emily's baby, she glanced over her shoulder to see exactly where he might be behind her and there he was, larger than life…a cowboy riding her way. Actually, galloping. On a horse. OK, so maybe not a *real* cowboy in the Western movie sense but he was certainly a doctor on a horse who gave her an unexpected chill. And he was also a big, imposing figure of a man. Jeans, T-shirt, boots. *Sexy.* "Other casualties?" he shouted, as he slid off the horse and ran straight towards her.

Deanna shook herself out of her observation, out of the pure fascination that was overrunning her, displacing the fugitive fantasy with the reality. "Um…don't know. We've got a car over the side, about two hundred yards back…" She pointed to the black skid marks snaking across the road for a hundred yard stretch. "And a truck. Don't know anything about the driver. Haven't had a chance to go over there to see him yet."

The doctor, Beau, crowded into the back seat of the car right behind her and nudged her forward most of the way to the opposite door then twisted around and proceeded to wedge himself between the back seat and the front. Doing his own assessments, as Deanna attempted to make herself more accessible to the boy, who'd curled even tighter into a ball.

After mere seconds he sucked in a sharp breath, which Deanna heard, and understood.

"How about we get the child out of here?" Beau asked. "There's nothing here he needs to see."

Even though she had been prepared to hear the words, the implication hit her hard. "Both of them?" she asked.

"Both of them." He began to back out of the car, pulling his massive form out of the too-small space. "How about you? Are you OK in there?"

"Don't have a choice," she said, as she began the struggle to lift the boy from the floor and at the same time assess him for injuries she might not have seen right off. The truth was, nothing about this was OK. But it wasn't about her feelings or memories. Or any inherent fears she might have for what this child was about to face.

"Then I'm going round to the truck. Janice Parsons, standing over at the minivan, said she'll look after the boy if we need her to, so shout if you need anything else, OK?"

If she needed anything else? She needed everything, including a way out of this. Her parents, Emily…it was all closing in around her. Smothering her. "Oh, and the dispatcher said she'd get the volunteer fire department out. But I don't know how long that's going to take."

"Too long," Beau shouted, his voice diminishing even before his words were all out. "Damn problem with all of this. It always takes too long!"

Deanna rose up and took a quick glance out the window, just enough to see him run behind the truck, and while she knew she wasn't alone here, that's how she felt. Amazing how twenty seconds crammed together in a car with him had bolstered her self-confidence.

"So, is your name Tommy?" she asked the child, as

she gently moved in to take his pulse. Strong, a little too fast. But he was scared. "Or Billy?" She wiggled her hand from his and brushed long, curly blond locks from his forehead, then took a look into his eyes as best she could. Pupils equal and reactive. "Or Porcupine?" Counted his respirations—normal.

"Not Porcupine," he finally said.

She was so relieved to hear his voice. "If it's not Porcupine, is it...Bulldog?"

"Not Bulldog," he said, tears welling up in his eyes.

She began a gentle prodding of his limbs, no heightened pain sensitivity noted. Then his belly. Not rigid, no distension. "Kangaroo?" she asked, trying to move him slightly to his side to make sure nothing was sticking into him in any way, like shards of glass from the shattered windshield or objects that might have flown around the car. But he was clear of everything, and she was beginning to wonder if he'd been curled up on the floor of the car when this had happened. Maybe asleep?

He whimpered something Deanna didn't understand but which she took to be him asking for his mommy. Glancing over the seat to the lifeless form, she drew in a ragged breath. "Mommy needs to rest right now. So does Daddy. So I'm going to open this car then we'll get out very quietly so we won't disturb them. Will you help me do that, Kangaroo?"

"Not Kangaroo."

"Is it Hippopotamus?" she asked, as she pushed on the car door then climbed out. "Or Walrus?"

Leaning back in, she scooped the boy into her arms and lifted him away from the wreckage, taking great care to make sure his face was buried in her shoulder. What an awful thing, seeing your parents that way and having that memory linger as your last memory of them. Her parents had died this way, in a car wreck. But she hadn't been in the car, and her very last recollection of them was the hugs and kisses they had given her when they'd dropped her off at her aunt and uncle's house. Hugs, kisses, and I love yous shouted from the car window as they'd pulled away from the curb… "I personally like Cheetah, or Chimpanzee."

"It's Lucas," the child said, but so quietly it was more a muffled sob than a word.

Did he know? Did he have some innate feeling that he'd just become an orphan? She hadn't when it had happened to her. In fact, it had taken months to sink in, months in which she'd spent every minute she could with her face pressed to the window, watching for them to come back.

Deanna didn't know about Lucas, though. Didn't know if he had an innate feeling, or just plain knew, because she didn't know a thing about children. She'd never been around them except for a few mandatory clinical rotations through pediatrics, and she'd certainly never planned on having them herself. She'd never been struck with that maternal urge the way Emily had. While it had defined her cousin, it had eluded her. So motherhood had never been included in her life plan—a decision she'd been fine with.

Of course, Emily's baby changed all that. Still, she wasn't consumed with an innate sense of motherhood the way she'd expected to be, the way she'd seen it in so many other women she'd known. The way Janice Parsons was when she bundled Lucas into her arms so protectively the instant Deanna handed him over to her.

"I think he's OK," she said, a little envious of the way the boy went from her embrace to someone else's so easily. Hadn't she snuggled him the right way? "His name is Lucas, and I'll have the doctor do another exam on him as soon as he can. In the meantime, if you could…"

There was no sense in finishing the sentence. Janice's

mothering instincts were on full alert as she turned Lucas away from the wreckage. All that natural tendency—a beautiful thing to see, really. "Don't give him anything to eat or drink," she said, taking one last look at the boy then at Janice, envying the way she exuded motherliness from every pore.

Would that ever be her?

That thought plagued her as she ran over to the edge of the road where the guardrail was smashed and broken, then looked down. Thank God, the drop-off to the first ledged area was barely more than a hundred feet. Sure, it was a long distance if you were in the car going over it, but the distance was short enough that she was cautiously optimistic.

"Hello," she shouted. "Can anybody hear me?"

The response was one staccato honk, which came as pure relief. But also frustration, knowing she couldn't make that climb down. Thank heavens some kind of natural instinct had kicked in and kept her planted on *terra firma*, because her natural inclination would have had her over the side before she'd even given it a thought. She still wondered, though, if that instinct would be enough in the long term because, dear God, everything in her wanted her to go over that edge.

"Help's on the way," she shouted, actually taking a step backwards. "Please, don't move. And if you have a cell-phone…" She called out her number and actually stood there for a second, waiting for a call back. Which didn't come. "I'm going to go get the doctor. We also have the fire department on the way. So don't give up. We're going to get you out of there in a few minutes."

"Truck driver's wedged," Beau said, the instant Deanna rounded the front of the truck. He was standing on the asphalt, looking through the windshield at the driver, who was stuck fast between the steering-wheel and the seat. "Internal injuries, some bleeding. Broken arm. Mangled leg…not sure if it can be saved. Head trauma but conscious. Strong possibility of hemorrhagic shock once we get him out. I can't do anything about it until we have more help.

"I'd stay in there with him but it's too tight and I don't want to risk slipping or moving the wrong way and hurting him more than he already is."

"We've got survivors in the car that went over," she said, trying to sound positive.

"Were you able to get down there?" he asked, his eyes glued to what was visible of the man in the truck.

"No, but someone honked."

"So all we need is…"

"Everything," Deanna said. "All we need is everything." She studied the man next to her for a moment. Mid-thirties, but with some lines etched in his face. Dark brown hair, a bit over the collar and wavy. Brown eyes. The kinds of things that would have been included on the sperm-donor card—had there been a donor card. But in addition to the sperm switch, the donor card had gone missing.

What wouldn't have been described on that card, though, was the kindness she saw in his eyes. From that, she was drawn in immediately. Not that his good looks alone couldn't have done it but those were an added bonus, gave her some hope for the way Emily's child might look. "My name is Deanna Lambert. But I'm betting you already knew that, didn't you?"

He smiled, although he didn't even glance in her direction. "You're renting a cabin here for a month to do some medical writing. Live in New York City otherwise."

"And my zodiac sign?"

He chuckled. "Give me ten more minutes and I'll not

only tell you your zodiac sign, I'll describe your high-school graduation in detail."

"That bad here?" she asked.

"Or good, depending on your point of view. The people here describe it as caring and, for the most part, I think that's right." Finally, he glanced at her, but for only a second. "I'm Beau Alexander, by the way. Local and possibly temporary doctor, aspiring horse breeder, mender of fences."

She'd known who he was, but hearing the name—*from him*—still shocked her, made her reason for being here even more real. Scared her, too. Most of all it made her feel sad, thinking about the way such a happy pregnancy was turning out. "I think I may be renting the cabin above your ranch."

"Above the Clouds. Nice view. Been up there a couple of—"

His words were cut off by the ringing of Deanna's cellphone, and without thinking she clicked it on. Listened for a second. Drew in a deep breath. "It's the people in the car," she said to Beau.

"What?"

"I gave them my cellphone number in case they wanted to call me. So they're calling."

"Damn," he muttered, impressed with her resourcefulness. More than that, impressed with everything he'd seen of her so far. "Good thinking."

"Only thing that came to mind. So, do you want to do this?"

He shook his head. "Got to stay focused on the driver, and I have to go back into the truck as soon as the fire department shows up and can keep the door open for me." The distant wail of several sirens caused him to sigh in relief.

"They're at Turner's Points now…you can tell by the echo. Turner's is the first place in the canyon that catches the sound like that. And it means they'll be here in about five minutes." He ran up to the truck windshield and gave the man a thumbs-up then turned back to Deanna, who was already on her way back to the side of the road where the car had gone over.

"Deanna," he shouted to her, "direct the medical end of the rescue when they get here, because when I get back into the truck I'm not getting out until after my patient does." Meaning he was going to have to wedge himself into a damned uncomfortable spot practically underneath the man, and stay put. He had to brace the man's leg, hopefully apply some kind of a splint, before they could move him, and at the same time keep his fingers crossed that the driver would survive the efforts to cut him out of there.

He glanced back at her, watched the way she instructed the paramedics who'd just arrived. He observed her body language, her no-nonsense stance, and liked her instantly. He wished he could have someone like her working alongside him every day.

"Hire someone like Deanna," he grunted, more to himself than out loud as he hauled himself up the side of the truck after two firefighters had dismantled the door for him and tossed it down on the road like it weighed no more than a plastic water bottle.

"Couldn't hurt," he said under his breath as he reached the top then started to lower himself back inside. "Might even help."

Considering the way he and his grandfather were battling over how to run a medical practice, he was pretty sure that having someone capable like Deanna involved would be another of the old man's objections. But Beau had to have his say in the matter if he was going to stay here permanently. And having a nurse or a medical assistant seemed like a good idea.

He'd known her for only a few minutes yet he wanted Deanna. Snap judgment and right fit, he believed. But he'd heard she was only renting for a month, which meant she wasn't staying in Sugar Creek. So now the problem was that Deanna had become the only person who flitted across his mind's eye when he thought about hiring another staffer. And she was such a nice fit he wasn't sure how to alter that image.

"Well, Mack, this ought to be pretty easy, once I get you splinted up," he said, trying to sound optimistic in order to bolster the truck driver's spirits.

"Don't think it's going to be easy, Doc. But I'm willing to give it a try. Need to be home later…wife's having a few friends over for dinner. It's my granddaughter's fifth birthday. Don't want to miss that."

"Just one granddaughter?" Beau asked, looking through the windshield at Deanna, still admiring what he saw. Striking woman. Tall. Hair the color of honey. Very subdued, though. Here, in the middle of this accident, showing so much command, she had such a sense of calmness about her. It baffled him because, as experienced as he was as a surgeon, he was still feeling the adrenalin rush.

"Just the one." he said. "Got a grandson, though, who just turned two. You a family man, Doc? You got kids?"

"Nope. Had a wife for a while. It didn't work out. Glad now we didn't get around to having children because she was…" he did a quick visual assessment of Mack as he climbed past him then lowered himself to a position almost underneath him "…selfish. And that's being kind." Pulling a flashlight from his pocket, he looked at the man's leg for a second time. Definitely a fractured tibia. Not mangled but also not good.

"Married her for her looks, got what I deserved because when you got past the looks all that was there was pure, unadulterated selfishness." For all intents and purposes.

"That bad, eh, Doc?"

"Bad doesn't even begin to describe it," Beau said, shifting position but trying to keep well away from his patient. Outside, he could hear the noise level increasing, multiple voices shouting. "Next time…" He drew in a shuddering breath. "No next time. At least, not for a long, long time."

Mack chuckled then sucked in a sharp breath. "I got lucky the first time out," he said, his voice noticeably weaker than it had been even a minute before. "Married the perfect woman, had thirty-five good years so far. Hoping I'll have a few…" Another gasp for air. "A few more."

I hope so too, Beau said to himself as a blanket dropped down from the door opening.

"Cover you two up," the burly voice shouted. "Windshield's coming out next."

Seconds after that the windshield had gone, and Beau was amazed by the speed with which everything was happening. He'd never worked a rescue from this end of it, and he wondered how many times over the years his grandfather had been called on to do something like this. It was a side of Brax he'd never considered, and he felt embarrassed that he hadn't. "Need a splint in here," he called. "And MAST trousers."

"What can I do from out here?" Deanna yelled to him from just beyond the front of the truck. "I've got rescuers setting up to go over the side right now to help the people in the car, and I'm not needed there until they bring them up. So what can I do for you in the meantime?"

"Oxygen, IV set-up…fast fluids."

"Already got them set up."

"Possible field amp." No way he was going to say "amputation" where the patient could hear, but if internal injuries didn't turn into an issue, the mangled leg might. "You OK with that?" he asked.

"Sure, I'm OK. I'll get everything together," she said, turning and running back to the rescue truck.

"She's a pretty one, too, Doc," Mack said, his voice almost gone now. "Better watch out."

Mack was right. Deanna was already fascinating him way more than she should. "Look, Mack, this is going to be a little tricky because of the way you're wedged in. Your right leg is pretty bad, and you might have a fractured pelvis. Not sure what we're going to do about those yet because I think you could also have some internal bleeding going on because of the way the steering-wheel is shoved into your belly."

He glanced up as one of the medics fresh to the scene dangled into the door opening, endeavoring to take the driver's blood pressure. "Since you're pressed so tight against the wheel, it's serving as a pressure bandage of sorts, keeping the blood circulating to your vital organs. But once the wheel is removed, there's a good chance you're going to experience a major internal hemorrhage." A mild understatement as once he was unwedged, the fight would be on to save him.

"So there's going to be some surgery in your future as soon as we can get you to the hospital. Right now, because you're in shock, you're not feeling so much pain. But in another minute, when we make the big move to get you out of here…I'm not going to lie to you. It's going to hurt like hell. But that pretty nurse out there's got an IV with your name on it, and she's ready to get some painkillers into you. Are you with me so far?"

"Doesn't sound like a picnic, Doc. But I'm with you."

"Good, because it's going to happen pretty fast now."

He watched Deanna direct the stretcher to just outside the truck then recheck the supplies laid out for this part of the rescue. Sill cool as the proverbial cucumber, she was the only one involved here who didn't seem frantic.

"Can I ask you one favor, Doc?"

"Sure. What is it?"

"Somewhere in the back I've got a birthday present for my granddaughter. However this turns out, would you see that she gets it?"

A lump formed in Beau's throat. "How about I save it for you to give to her?" he said. "And I'll tell her to save you some birthday cake."

"Appreciate it, Doc. Now, if you don't mind, I need to call my wife…"

"You talk while I splint your leg and get you ready to move." He didn't want to hear the conversation, it would be too personal.

So he bit his lower lip hard to create a distraction for himself and quickly splinted Mack's lower leg, trying to block out the way Mack was trying to be supportive to his wife even though he was the one in critical condition. Trying to block out thoughts of Nancy, who didn't have it in her to think of anyone but herself in a critical situation.

Pulling the last elastic bandage into place around Mack's splint, Beau started to withdraw himself from the cab to allow the standby firefighters and medics their turn with him. "OK, let's get you out of here and on the next helicopter to the hospital. You with me?"

Mack's cellphone dropped to the floor, which was actually the passenger-side door, and as Beau twisted to grab it for him, he saw the wrapped birthday present and grabbed it as well. Something soft, a stuffed animal, he guessed.

"Deanna," he yelled, then tossed it out for her to catch. "Mack, cross your arms over your chest and let the med-

ics do all the work. And, please, don't fight against them."
After one last check to make sure Mack was as stable as
possible, Beau unwedged himself all the way and practically poured out of the front of the truck, bouncing off the
hood then hitting the ground with a thump, landing rather
ungraciously on his bum right at Deanna's feet.

"You OK?" she asked, extending a hand to him to help
him up.

"No, I'm not," he snapped, taking hold of her hand—
such soft skin—and righting himself. "Sorry. I'm OK, but
my patient…" He shrugged then looked back at the truck
as the firefighters cut away large chunks of the truck to
get at its driver.

"Look, Beau, I don't do this too often…patient care.
Especially trauma and field rescue. But I understand the
basics, we're as ready for him as we can be. So just tell
me what I need to be doing."

He nodded. "What about the car that went over?"

"Both people inside are injured, one conscious, one
not. Until the rescuers get into the car, we won't know
any more."

"OK, then." He looked at the MAST trousers, which
Deanna had laid out on the ground and opened up all the
way. They were essentially the same as a blood-pressure
cuff, with all the same sticky fasteners, gauges and tubes
running in and out to blow them up. If knowing how to get
them ready was what Deanna called the basics, she was
greatly underestimating herself. "Let's do this."

Giving a nod to the rescuers in the truck, who were
awaiting his direction, Beau stepped away from the trousers to allow the rescuers a clear path then turned to watch
them cut away the steering-wheel and dashboard, almost
in the blink of an eye.

In that same blink of an eye his patient ripped out the

most blood-curdling scream imaginable. Beau drew in a shuddering breath and felt the squeeze of Deanna's hand on his arm. "I hate this," he whispered. "Damn, I hate this."

"I've got morphine ready."

Another awful scream and her squeeze tightened. "If he lives that long."

"He'll live that long." Deanna dropped to her knees as the firefighters ran forward and laid the driver directly atop the open trousers. Immediately she began to pull one of the legs over Mack's left leg, while Beau did the same with the right, and in a fraction of a second, they were both closing the fasteners.

There was another scream from Mack but this one weaker, and at the end of it he passed out. "Stay with us," Beau said, as he pumped pressure into the trousers. "You've got birthday cake to eat."

"Birthday cake?" Deanna asked, without diverting her attention from the site she was cleaning on Mack's arm for an IV.

"His granddaughter's birthday. You're not bad for a writer, by the way. Pretty good skill sets in the field."

"Not bad for a writer who's putting an IV in someone who doesn't have a blood pressure," Deanna corrected, then smiled as she slid the needle into the vein near the crook of Mack's left arm.

"Do you like working trauma?" he asked, still astounded by her efficiency.

After she had taped the IV in place, she glanced over at Beau, who was listening to heart and breath sounds. "Don't dislike it. Not sure I'd want a steady diet of it, though." Returning her attention to her patient, she attached the IV tubing then hooked that to a bag of Ringer's, which would help replace fluid volume lost through bleeding. "And you?"

"Surgeon, by training. Country GP...by obligation. Maybe by choice, but I haven't made up my mind yet."

"Ah, two diverse worlds with just as diverse appeals." She signaled for the medic to hand her an oxygen mask then placed it on Mack's face.

"Maybe too diverse," he said, leaning over Mack to check his eyes for pupillary response. "Not sure where I fit yet."

"Which is why you're here?"

"I'm here because my grandfather isn't able to manage his practice any longer, and there's no one else to take care of his patients until I decide if I want to stay or bring somebody else in. He needed me, even though the old coot isn't about to admit it."

"Am I sensing family discord?"

"More like family stubbornness." He pushed himself away from Mack, then stood up and waved for the medics to take the man. "Not such an endearing trait, I've been told."

"So now what?" she asked, as she also stood, then stepped back. "An hour or so to the hospital? Will he be able to do that in his condition"

"Less, by helicopter."

"If you can get one. Airlift in areas such as this isn't always convenient when you need it."

"Unless you own a helicopter."

She arched her eyebrows. "I'm impressed."

"I was too when my grandfather bought it. Not so much now that I have to fly it."

"You fly?"

He shrugged. "Somebody has to. But normally I sit in the back with the patient and let Joey do the flying. He manages the ranch, tends the horses and my grandfather, flies the chopper." Something about her made him lose all caution, and just when he thought he'd perfected the fine art of keeping his privacy at all costs. Another pretty face, he decided. Like Mack had said—watch out!

"So we'll transport Mack to your helicopter, and..."

"And hope the people they're going to bring up from over the edge can make do with an hour's ride in the back of an ambulance."

"You really are deprived out here, aren't you?"

"Not deprived," he said, not so much offended by her remark as curious about it. "Slowed down, forced to be inventive."

"My mistake," she said, following Beau, who was running along behind the medics who were ready to load Mack into the back of an ambulance that would transport him to the Alexander landing strip.

"Logical conclusion. Look, you handle the rest of it. I've got to go." Which was exactly what he did. He climbed into the ambulance with Mack then watched Deanna until the doors shut on him. Even then, he stared through the tiny window until she was but a speck in the distance.

Deanna Lambert... Their paths had been meant to cross, he decided. He didn't know why, didn't even know what kind of medical writing she did. But it didn't matter. Something had just started, and while he didn't know what it was, he was anxious to find out.

CHAPTER THREE

"NICE VIEW OF my grandfather's ranch," Beau said, settling into the porch chair next to Deanna. He stretched out his long legs. "He used to hate it that someone up here could sit and watch what he was doing. But then he discovered the beauty of a good pair of binoculars and while I haven't seen him actually watching anybody up here, I think it gives him a certain sense of satisfaction knowing he can look up as well as they—or you—can look down."

"I don't blame him. I don't like being watched either. I spent a lot of my youth having people looking at me, trying to figure out what to do with me, and now I like to keep to myself."

"And yet you're a nurse?"

"Not in the sense most people would think of it but, yes, I'm a nurse." They were seated on the north porch this morning, watching the emerging new day and trying to forget all the haunting, hideous memories from yesterday.

Her parents had died in a car wreck. Then Emily had asked, "*Deanna, can I come stay with you for a few days? Alex and I had a fight and I may leave him for good.*" Rainy day, emotions overpowering rational thought, horrible outcome. Deanna cringed, reliving it, not sure she ever wanted to get into another car. So she fixed her attention on the vast forest she could see from her porch. Concentrated on something pleasant, for herself but mostly for the baby. "This is lovely, though, isn't it? So many trees. Nature everywhere you look."

Beau chuckled. "Sounds like you've been cooped up too much."

"I get out, it's always about work, though. Never really have much time to relax and when I do, my view at home is the rooftop next door. From just the right position, which is my left shoulder pressed to the wall with my neck cranked to a forty-five-degree angle, I can look out of one of my windows and see part of the city skyline. But I usually come away with sore muscles if I do that so I keep my curtains closed."

Of course, when she returned, she would have a new apartment, something a little farther away from the city. Maybe in a suburb, with nice playgrounds and lots of children.

Beau chuckled. "I lived in a place like that once. In medical school. One room, with a bathroom so small you had to sidestep into the shower. There were two windows, total—one with a view of the street and one with a view of a flashing red neon sign: *'Ralph's Packaged Liquors'*. During the day, though, when it was turned off, from the right angle you could see a little park at the end of the block, with some trees. Sometimes I'd catch myself standing there, just staring at trees. I had all the trees in the world right here, never even saw them."

It was pleasant just relaxing, enjoying the morning. And it seemed so natural it nearly made her forget she was sitting here with the baby's father. Never mind that for the moment, she decided. She simply wanted to enjoy his company. Everything else could come later. "We all do that, I think. Take the easy, dependable things in our lives for

granted. But I'm not taking this view for granted. It's spec-
tacular. I could sit here for hours and just look at...*trees*."

"And I have an idea down there, somewhere amongst
those trees, someone might be looking up here. Brax is
too idle these days, doesn't have enough to keep him busy,
and he got that little glint in his eyes when I told him I was
going to drop in on you."

Impulsively, she waved in the direction of the Alexander ranch. "You should have brought him along."

"He's a stubborn old bastard. Fought the development
up here when it happened, claimed it wouldn't be good for
his patients. And as far as I know, he's never been up here."

"Then he's missing out, because the view of his ranch is
stunning. Even though from here you look like ants." She
shifted, tucked her feet up under her, thought she could get
used to this. "So, any word from the hospital?"

"Mack, the truck driver, did well in surgery. They saved
his leg, removed his spleen, took out part of his liver. Put
him in traction for his pelvis. Tough road ahead for him,
lots of rehab in his future, but he's got a good family, a
huge family, actually, and they'll get him through it."

And all she had was this baby. Amazing, though, how
the developing life inside her connected her to so much
more than she could have ever expected. She and the baby
might not be a large family but they'd be a good family.
"Did he get any of that birthday cake?"

Beau chuckled. "Not yet. His family decided to put off
the birthday celebration until he's able to eat solid food
again."

"Good family," she said, truly glad for the man. "And
the other couple? The ones who went over the edge?"

"Lucky all the way around for them. A few sprains,
strains and bruises. Husband went home this morning, but
they're keeping the wife an extra day because she had a

slight concussion. And Lucas is fine, too. Social Services is looking for relatives who can take him in, but right now he's still with Janice Parsons, the minivan driver you gave him to, and she's going to keep him until other arrangements are made. So, how are you doing? That was a lot of effort for your first day in Sugar Creek. You look tired."

"First day? More like first hour. And, yes, I'm tired. Didn't sleep much last night, which means I'm paying the price for it this morning." Stretching her back, she stifled a yawn. "But basically I'm OK. What brings you up here this early other than to see if I'm spying on your ranch? Don't you have patients to see?"

"I save my mornings for…well, I'll admit it. I spend time with my horses. Childhood passion I'm getting to indulge now that I've come back to Sugar Creek. So barring a heavy schedule or an emergency, I block out a couple of morning hours to spend time in the stables. And if there's nothing pressing for the next hour or so, I like to do physical work on the ranch. The medical practice comes first, of course, but I believe in balance in all things, and a good part of my balance is tied to the ranch. Oh, and I do house calls in the evenings."

"Seriously? You make house calls?"

"Comes with the job when your medical practice is so spread out. It's necessary out here, and it gives me a chance to get off the ranch. It's especially nice if I can ride my horse."

"Tennessee cowboy doctor," she commented. The image of him on a horse was…nice. "In some parts of the medical world you'd be laughed at for your old-school ways."

"I have a surgical practice in New York and I can pretty well guarantee my patients there wouldn't care to see me ride up on my horse."

At his mention of New York a chill shot up her spine.

That got her right back to his sperm donation—in a New York clinic—and the fact that she was carrying his baby. All of it a wet blanket effect that caused her to straighten up on the swing, kick off the casual stance and don the starched one. "Yet here you are in Sugar Creek, being a country GP. How is that working out for you?"

"Let's just say I'm still getting used to it. Still trying to get myself settled into it after almost a year. And still trying to figure out whether or not I'll succeed in it, as part of me is still city surgeon. But all that said, I do like the lifestyle I have here. I've never worked harder in my life, and never had such a sense of…freedom."

Was this a good idea? Sitting here, actually getting to know the baby's father—when her only intention had been to come here and observe from afar, maybe sample some of the local flavor and hope to pick up a few tidbits about him as she did. Never had she planned on…well, this!

Deanna, I don't know what to do. I just got a phone call from the clinic. The baby you're carrying isn't Alex's. There was a name mix-up. Similar names, I think.

Emily's words had started a nightmare that had ended right here in Sugar Creek, on the porch, sitting comfortably next to her. "Yet you don't know if you're staying or going?"

"I love it here. Always have. But loving it and settling down here are two different things and I'm not sure if I'm cut out to be a country doctor for the rest of my life. In fact, I'd never really thought much past New York until I got the call that Brax had had a stroke and I was needed home for a while." He shrugged. "You do what you have to do, and for now this is what I have to do."

"Well, New York certainly has its charms." Charms she loved probably as much as Beau did. So she could understand his conflict. Uprooting a life was never easy and most of the time it came with a lot of trepidation. She'd had her fair share of that, although not so much now that she was here, enjoying the cabin, enjoying the view. Even enjoying the company of Emily's baby's daddy.

"So does Sugar Creek. Different charms, though, depending on what you want from your life. But things change. People change. Life changes and you either stay even with it or you get left behind."

"But can you really ever get ahead of it?" That had never been the case for her, but her life was different now and she hoped that somehow, some way she could get ahead of it. Lead the situation rather than allowing the situation to lead her. That's what coming to Sugar Creek was really about. Her attempt to get ahead of it. Finding out everything she could about Emily's baby's father was what would help her do just that.

Getting to know Beau Alexander was where she had started. That push in the right direction.

"Better to spend your time trying than falling further and further behind, I suppose. So now all I have to do is convince myself that settling down here in Sugar Creek isn't the same thing as getting left behind, and I'll be good. Although a year into the quest and I'll have to admit that the things I want to keep ahead of are changing."

"Sounds to me like you're trying to reconcile yourself to staying."

He sighed heavily but it was a contented sigh, not one out of exasperation. "Maybe I am. Duty calls, you know. And it's a pretty strong call when there's no one else to take care of the people around here. Besides, I owe it to Brax to do the right thing for him. He was the stalwart force in my life when everything else was going to hell and for that reason the adjustments aren't as difficult as they might be otherwise."

"You call your grandfather by his name?"

"There weren't any women in our lives...not for very long anyway. So we never stood on formalities. Al was my dad. Brax my grandfather... We're both Braxton Beauregard Alexander. And I'm the ninth in line to get the name."

"Braxton Alexander," she said. Alexander Braxton— Braxton Alexander. Sure, there was an uncanny similarity of names, but mixing them up? *Having a baby this way was Emily's idea, not mine. So do any damned thing you want, Deanna. Keep it, get rid of it. It's not mine and I don't care.* Even now, remembering Alex's words chilled her to the bone.

"Look Deanna, I didn't come up here to bore you all the details of my family name or how I need to decide what I'm going to do with my life. When Brax heard there was a pretty young nurse staying in the cabin, he insisted I come and invite you to breakfast, so...consider yourself invited.

"And as I said, we don't stand on formality around here. You're welcome to wander down the mountain for any meal we put on the table. No invite necessary." He grinned. "Unlike back in New York, where you'd probably be admitted for a psych evaluation for showing up unannounced and without an invitation."

"My New York's not that rigid. But, then, I don't encompass much of New York in my interests or lifestyle so that pretty well limits me. That, or we just run in different circles."

"Funny. I didn't take you for the kind of person who would limit herself in anything."

"There are lots of different kinds of limits, Beau. I think I've chosen mine to fit what I need."

"But what about what you want?"

Deanna thought about that for a moment, pondered the many things she wanted but wouldn't allow herself to have.

Ultimately, what you wanted hurt the most when you lost it and, in her experience, she always lost it. So why invest in her wants when the outcome was a given?

OK, so that was the dreary side of life showing itself, but in this case dreary was practical. It worked. And there was no need for him to know any of this because he was now, in some inexplicable fashion, tied up in her list of wants. She wanted to be around him, get to know him. Make sense of him so she could come to know Emily's baby in some way. "What I want? Right now, it's to get to work. It's not getting done with me sitting out here staring at the morning."

"All work, no play should make you hungry, so how about that breakfast invitation?"

She was hungry, she had to admit. But to insert herself into the heart of the Alexander clan? Although Beau's grandfather was family to this baby, too. But this was too much, too soon. "I, um…I appreciate the offer. But, like I said…"

"Your book awaits."

"No, not a book. More like a report. I'm a nurse researcher, and I work for a group of physicians who have a very specific vision about getting better healthcare to places that don't have it. You know, rural populations, isolated areas. So to that end I do the preliminary research, write the papers and journal articles that will bring in the financial donors for various projects. Sometimes I lecture, and every other semester I teach a class."

"Sounds complicated."

"Not really. Not when you know what you're doing."

"And you're pretty good?"

"I'm pretty good."

"Like the Ellerby Project in West Virginia, where you

found funding for Dr. Louis Ellerby to start a clinic in an area that hasn't seen convenient healthcare in a century?"

"You've read about me?"

"About your work. Last night at the hospital, while I waiting for Mack to come out of surgery. Although I'll admit I did some internet searching on you and came up with...practically nothing."

That was a relief. She was still concerned, though, that he'd been digging around into her past, as bland as it was. Although turnabout was fair play, since she'd been digging into his past. "Just the way I like it." She was a little uncomfortable, though, knowing he was *looking* at her.

"Being in the background?"

"Not in the background. As often as not I get to implement one of my projects and see it come to life. But I don't like...fuss."

"Are you here in Sugar Creek to *fuss*? You know, find a problem with our healthcare and fix it?"

It hadn't occurred to her he might think that. Or that her presence here could look like she was on a project. "No, I'm here to... I just needed time away from the city. I've got some decisions to make about my future, sort of like what you're doing, and I'm in the middle of a move when I get back home. So, basically, I needed a break. Sugar Creek seems the perfect place for that and, as far as I can see, it's in good hands, medically speaking. You may be spread too thin, but compared to some of the places I've been..."

Suddenly, Beau sat bolt upright and twisted to face her. "Work for me," he interrupted, not sure why he'd just made the offer. "I know you didn't come here to work, and I'm not even sure why I'm asking. But I am. So, come and work for me, Deanna."

"What? I mean...I don't understand."

"You look for solutions, and I need to see if a nurse, or

even a second doctor, would be my solution here. And I don't mean full time. Just spend a couple hours a day in the clinic to see some of the lesser cases. Maybe a house call or two. To see if my problem can be fixed."

"Your problem?"

"A grandfather who doesn't want anybody in the practice. He's old-school, a one-man show. And critical of how I'm running his practice. The thing is, for me to stay here I've got to find a way to appease him and still run things the way I need to, and right now I'm drowning. He says it's because I'm unfocused, but I say it's because we exist in two different medical worlds, and that the day of the solitary GP is over. Medicine has more, it's expanded since Brax was my age, and while in knowledge it hasn't left him behind, in practice it has.

"But I have to prove that to him, let him see something that makes him understand that I have to do things my way or I won't be able to stay here. Then Sugar Creek turns into one of those problems you're sent to solve."

"And with me working for you…"

"You'll see both sides, where he's wrong, where I'm wrong. That's what I need."

"Then you think he's entirely wrong and you're entirely right? Is that the premise I have to work with if I take this on?"

Of course he was right. But he just didn't know where he was wrong or else he'd fix it. "Let's just say Brax and I share a certain stubbornness, which is probably working against both of us."

"No probably about it. Too much ego hurts the practice."

He chuckled. "See, that's what I mean. We need that kind of observation. And I'm willing to pay for it. I read about this clinic you're trying to expand in Wyoming. It needs a small surgery. Work for me, and it's funded."

"Just like that? I give you a few hours and you give me a surgery?"

"And a new exam room. The article said you wanted to expand by adding one more exam room."

Well, one thing was certain. He was catching her attention with his offer. "You know how to make a hard-to-refuse offer, don't you?"

"Well, I thought about it, rejected it, thought about it again, and…" He shrugged. "Never hurts to try."

"I'm not even sure I've got time…"

"Make time," he said earnestly. "Whatever you can spare. Work any time you're able, fit it into your schedule, not mine."

"As tempting as this is, you have to know one thing. If I do this, and I'm not saying I will, but if I do I'll be fixing a professional problem," she warned. "Not a personal one between you and your grandfather. That's for you two to sort out."

But with the professional fix would come the personal fix, he hoped. He really did love the old guy, but loving him and trying to run his medical practice were two entirely different things. And their problems with the practice were beginning to affect their relationship.

"You're right. It is. But it's complicated, Deanna, because it's hard to separate one from the other. If we can get the problems with the practice sorted and come to some kind of understanding, I'm sure Brax and I will go back to normal. So, yes, all professional."

"Before I commit to anything, let me ask you one simple question. Do you want to stay here? You sound like someone who does, yet I'm sensing a streak of resistance."

It wasn't a simple question, because he was torn. He'd hoped, when he'd come home, that his sentiments would swing harder one way or the other while he was here, but that hadn't happened. And he was down to the wire now.

His partners wanted him back or they wanted his resignation so they could turn their temporary replacement for him in to a permanent member of the staff. And the medical practice here needed someone who could make the firm commitment. So, no, that wasn't a simple question at all. In fact, it was the hardest one he'd ever had to think over.

"Ideally, I could have both worlds—the one I have in New York and the one I'm trying to find here. That said, I know I can't, so my preference would be..." He shrugged. "That's what I'm trying to find out because I'm really straddling the fence."

"Like personal heart in one place and professional heart in another?"

"See, you do understand."

"The easy decision would be to flip a coin. Then you wouldn't have to buy me a new exam room and a surgical suite in Wyoming." She smiled. "Although getting that exam room and surgery would *so* uncomplicate my life right now. Save me half the work I brought with me to do."

"Which means you'll do it because you're about to have some spare time?"

"Which means I'll think about it. That's all I can say right now."

"Then how about you think about it over breakfast, and meet Brax?"

"I do have to eat, don't I? It's good for the..." She broke off her words and sighed as she glanced down the mountain then waved at the old man again, in case he was watching. "Good for me. It's good for *me*."

That's when Beau saw her drift away for a moment, thinking about something else, something profoundly sad and far away. It was perceptible in her eyes. In the way her shoulders slumped. He understood anger, and rage. He'd lived his entire life with an undertow of restlessness and discontent.

But sadness hadn't touched him, except for that one moment when he'd realized that his marriage had been about betrayal, not commitment. And even then that sadness had turned into intense distrust. But the sadness he saw in her...he didn't understand it. It was so deep, and so close.

"Before I meet him, will he be good with this, Beau? Your grandfather? Will he accept an outsider coming in and making suggestions as he's resisting *your* suggestions?"

"If you work for me, you won't be an outsider. And he's not an ogre. Just stubborn. But he'll listen to you because..."

"Because I don't share his stubbornness, like you do."

"You have a way with words," he said, standing up. "Very direct."

She laughed. "Very direct, and no partiality. As they say in today's vernacular, that's the way I roll."

Well, he was beginning to like the idea that Deanna had rolled into his life, even if it was only his professional life. Working with her for a while, whatever the reason, would be nice. For her nursing skills.

And maybe the pleasure of her company. Because he sure did like that as well.

Deanna refused yet another biscuit as she shoved away her plate. "That was amazing," she said, as Vera Holland, the Alexander housekeeper, tried ladling one last scoop of fresh fruit into Deanna's bowl. "But I can't eat another bite...for a week."

Brax laughed out loud. "You eat breakfast with us often enough and you'll see just how small your appetite is compared to the rest of us. Beau's slowed down, though, since he's been back."

"I like bagels," Beau defended. "Got used to them when I lived in New York. Give me a good, fresh poppyseed bagel, some cream cheese..."

Brax snorted. "City ways."

"Maybe, but your country ways will make me fat and lethargic. And, Deanna, we don't usually eat like this... eggs, bacon, biscuits, grits... It was going to be simple until I told Brax who you were and what you might do to help us, then he decided put on the spread to impress you because he wants to lure you over to his side."

"His side?" she asked setting down her glass of fresh orange juice. "How so?"

"My grandson doesn't think the way I ran my medical practice is good enough," Brax cut in.

Brax bit the inside of his cheek to stop himself from saying something he'd regret. Loving the old man was one thing, but too often lately tolerating him was difficult. Instead, he looked over at Deanna, who gave him a barely perceptible nod, like she understood. "What I think, Brax, is that I need to get out to the stables for a few minutes. If Deanna would care to join me..."

"You've avoiding the issue," the old man warned him.

"Not avoiding it. Just skirting around it until later."

"Now or later. We've got to deal with this, son."

"Which is why I'm here," Deanna chimed in. "To sort it out and hope you both listen to me."

"Then you've decided to do it?" Beau asked, glad and surprisingly excited. Holding the emotion in reserve, of course. "You've decided to work here for a while?"

"I think it's probably the best way to get up close and personal with the both of you. And stay impartial." She gave Brax a particularly pointed glance on that note. "So, yes, for a little while."

"Excellent. I think we'll have hotcakes for breakfast tomorrow morning," Brax said enthusiastically.

"I think I'll have yogurt, alone in my cabin tomorrow morning," Deanna countered as she scooted way from the table and gathered up her dishes. "Working here is one thing but fraternizing is another, if I want to be objective. And I want to be objective."

For the first time in weeks it felt like half the load had been lifted from his shoulders, and Beau was grateful for that. Grateful for Deanna stepping in. Honestly, he didn't know if there was anything she could really do about solving the problem here, but just having her understand and evaluate it made him feel ten times better. Gave him some hope.

Because on the surface, the problem looked pretty grave. The old man had practically raised him. Brax had turned his life inside out to always be there for a sad little boy who'd had an irresponsible father. And yet now, when his grandfather needed his patience and understanding, it seemed like he didn't have enough of it to give.

The compromises should have come easier, but they hadn't. The communication between them should have been better, but it wasn't. So, was this something Deanna, an outsider, could fix, or even nudge along in the right direction? Hell if he knew. But he was relieved more than he'd thought he would be because she just… He glanced at her walking into the kitchen with an armload of dishes, then noticed the twinkle in his grandfather's eyes. Deanna just fit. That's what it was. She just fit.

"You've got that look, Beau," Brax commented once Deanna was out of earshot.

"What look?"

"*That* look. One I used to see in you from time to time before you married the shrew."

"You mean admiration for a pretty girl? Hell, yes, I have it. Deanna's easy on the eyes."

Brax chuckled. "If that's what you want to tell yourself, fine. She's easy on the eyes. I'll agree. But that look… you're thinking of her in different terms, aren't you?"

"I'm thinking of her as the nurse who's going to drum some sense into that thick skull of yours, old man." He gave his grandfather an affectionate squeeze on the shoulder then headed for the door. "When she comes out of the kitchen, tell her I'm out on the porch, and I'd like her to join me."

"Like I said," Brax said.

"Like you said…nothing. Leave it alone, Brax. OK? Just leave it alone." Easier said than done. Because his grandfather did care, did want Beau to be happy.

No more than Beau himself did, though. Absolutely no more than Beau did.

"He's…" The word wasn't *stubborn*, even though Brax was stubborn. But she didn't want to be insulting because she liked the man. Saw a lot of Beau in him. "Formidable. Very strong-willed."

Beau chuckled. "You're trying to be nice."

"Maybe I am, but I like him, Beau. He's a lot like you. Or, should I say, you're a lot like him."

"I've been called worse."

Propped casually against the porch rail, leaning back against it yet not sitting, arms folded across his chest, feet crossed at the ankles…he was stunning. Especially with the way the morning sun kindled golden highlights in his otherwise dark brown hair.

He had a hard, chiseled look to him, and contrasted with

Emily's softness, her pale skin and blonde hair, Deanna was sure the baby would be beautiful with the looks of either parent. Or both. "It's a compliment. And you're lucky to have him, Beau, stubborn or not."

"Don't know what I'd do without him," he admitted. "My mom died when I was a baby, and my dad spent most of my formative years trying to forget he had a kid. So Brax was the one who got me through the rough patches, especially when I was on the verge of turning into a juvenile delinquent."

"You were not!" she exclaimed.

"Worst kid in Sugar Creek. Ask anybody who remembers me. If there was trouble, I was either instigating it or in the middle of it." He smiled fondly. "I can remember maybe five or six times when Brax had to go down to the jail to get me out. And I'm not talking a hardened teenager getting thrown into jail. First time for me I was ten. I'd set one of the Founders' Day parade floats on fire."

So the baby would probably come with some feistiness. That was good to know.

"And they arrested you even though you were only ten?"

"More like locked me up until the parade was over so I didn't get into any more trouble. Then I got to wash Mr. Gentry's front window—he owned the bakery—once a week for a year because it was his float I burned down."

"And yet you didn't learn your lesson, did you?"

"About fires, yes. Didn't set another one. But there were other incidents. Mrs. Duncan's favorite porch rocker mysteriously ending up in the top of a tree. Mr. Baxter's car parked in Miss Monroe's front yard one morning…he was the very married school principal, she was the very single kindergarten teacher who was having an affair with him. Little town scandal revealed because I'd learned how to hotwire a car. Oh, and all the fire hydrants on Main Street being painted pink one night. To name a few incidents."

OK, so maybe feisty wasn't quite the best way to describe it. Creative. Yes, he was creative. A very appealing trait she would most definitely have to direct in the baby. "You terrorized the poor little town, yet look at you smile."

"I smiled then, too, until I got thrown into jail. Then it was all frowns and shaking because I knew what Brax would do when he came to get me out."

"What?"

"Hard physical labor. Mending fences, cutting back the brush line. Back-breaking work for anybody, and almost impossible for someone young and scrawny, like I was."

She had a hard time imagining him scrawny. "Yet you were a repeat offender."

"That I was."

"And if I were a psychologist, I'd say there was definitely a pattern there. Some kind of emotional process you were trying to work out."

"If you were a psychologist, you'd probably be right. But you're not. You're the nurse who's going to fix another of my problems."

"Who's going to *try* and fix another of your problems. No guarantees. I'll do the best I can, but I'm dealing with two very stubborn men who, I guess, have a long history of inflexibility. Am I right?"

He pushed away from the porch rail and glanced down toward the stables. "Care for a morning ride?"

OK, so he may not have answered her question, but his lack of an answer spoke volumes. No, it shouted. But she liked challenges. And the father of the baby she was carrying was definitely going to present her with a huge challenge.

"Sounds lovely, but no. I've got to get back to my cabin.

You're not the only one who employs me, and I've got some calls to make." But a ride around the ranch might have been nice had she ever been on a horse before or had she not been pregnant. "And if you want me to work a few hours in your clinic every day, I've got to get a jump on everything else when I can. But I appreciate the offer. Oh, and so you'll know, I'll take on some house calls with you. That actually sounds fascinating. But not on horseback."

"I have an SUV, if that works for you? Or a truck, or my self-indulgent little sports car my grandfather calls an abomination to four wheels and a drive shaft. Take your pick."

"An SUV is just fine. Or walking, if it's not too far."

"Whatever you wish. But the horse option is always open."

What she wished for was a healthy baby. What she also wished for was getting to know the baby's father. Simple things. At least, she hoped they were simple.

Suddenly, nothing seemed simple. Not one blessed thing in her life.

CHAPTER FOUR

IF HE DIDN'T stop staring up at her cabin, he wasn't going to get anything done. Two of the horses still needed their morning workout, and there was a fence section out on the back forty he hadn't gotten to and probably wouldn't for a day or two. There was too much to do to kill time the way he'd been doing this morning.

Sure, it was all hands-on work he could have Joey or someone else do, but one of the reasons he liked being back here was that he got to flex different muscles. He'd done it when he'd been young, gotten himself all buff doing it. Then medical school and even during his short tenure as general surgeon in New York had changed all that. No more tough physical work. No more ripped muscles. He'd grown soft. Too soft, without the necessary hours to remedy the abdomen that was no longer a six-pack and the pecs that weren't quite as firm.

It hadn't mattered because he hadn't cared. Being on the margin of well toned had been good enough. Now he wanted to be toned and perfect again, the way he'd been a decade ago. No reasons or excuses necessary, and he sure as hell wasn't conceding the coincidence of Deanna's arrival. It was simply time, that was all.

So, after years of relying on his brain rather than his brawn, he was being hit by this sudden urge to work himself back into shape, and this was where he could do that. But not if he kept standing here, staring up at her cabin.

"She's not up there, if that's what you're looking for. I saw her in town when I came through a while ago."

"I'm not looking for her," Beau said, even though that's exactly what he'd been doing. "Just…resting." At eleven in the morning. Like Joey was going to believe that.

"Well, looking or not, she's the prettiest woman I've seen around here in a long time. Sure glad the one you married the first time didn't ruin you for something else in the future." He glanced up the incline to the cabin and smiled. "Like the pretty little nurse you're *not* hoping to see."

Beau turned to face him. "Everybody knew Nancy was bad except me. Would have been nice if somebody had mentioned that to me before I married her."

"No, sir. You were staring cross-eyed at her, and it's not smart to come between a man and the woman he's looking at that way."

"Live and learn," Beau muttered, anxious to get off the subject. He didn't like talking about Nancy or thinking about her. "So let me get back to the horses. Onyx still needs a ride, so does Cashew, and I'm running out of time. I've got patients coming in early today."

"You're running out of time because you've been staring too long at her cabin." Joey chuckled. "And didn't she just leave here three hours ago?"

Beau dug deep for a comeback that would silence the man on the subject once and for all, but when nothing was forthcoming, Joey forged ahead. "Anyway, only because I think it's time you do more than stare, I'll exercise the horses and you can get yourself ready to see her when she comes to work later on. You know, get all primpy in front of the mirror…"

His chuckle turned into a belly laugh as he spun around and headed off in the opposite direction.

"I don't primp," Beau yelled after him.

"Neither do I," Deanna said, entering the stable from the other direction. "Decided a long time ago that with me it's the natural look or nothing."

Beau spun around to face her. "You're early."

"Actually, you never specified an exact time. So I'm neither early nor late. But I got everything done I needed to this morning, ran to the store in town, and decided to come here instead of going back up to the cabin for another hour or so."

Her gait was deliberately cautious and slow on the straw as she approached Beau. And so sexy he caught himself staring again.

"My first patient's due in about an hour, but you can work the hours that are best for your schedule. I'm grateful, not picky." His eyes darted to Joey, who popped back into the doorway behind Deanna, grinned, and gave him a thumbs-up. "But since you're here, I think it would be a good time to get yourself familiar with our medical set-up."

"Just point me to your fleams and blood-letting cups," she teased, referring to antique medical devices.

"We're a century or so past that," he said, laughing as he pulled a handful of sugar from his pocket then walking over to Nell's stall, where the heavily pregnant horse stretched her neck out to take it from his hand. "But sometimes I don't think so."

"Ah, that would be your attempt to sway me? Or, at least, prejudice me? And without the offer of future breakfasts?"

"How about the offer of dinner after our last house call this evening? Would that work for you?"

"We have a house call?"

"Five, if you want to go with me."

"I'll go, but not by horse. Remember?"

She walked up to Nell and stroked her muzzle, and moved in closer when she discovered the mare was as gentle as a kitten. Which put her in almost intimate proximity to Beau. He could smell her shampooed hair, feel the heat her body radiated. She was oblivious, standing there, making up to Nell. But he wasn't oblivious. In fact, he was so aware of her every nuance he had to take a step back. "Not by horse," he managed to say, hoping his voice didn't sound too adolescently squeaky.

"They're beautiful animals, though," she said, holding out her hand to him for some lumps of sugar. "I've always liked horses…in literature and movies. Never ridden one, being the city girl that I am, but I always thought I might like to learn someday. So, if I feed her this sugar she won't bite my hand, will she?"

He surrendered the sugar carefully, dropping each of the four lumps precisely, one by one, into her open palm so he didn't come into too much contact with her. "She's the soul of gentleness. Probably the sweetest horse I've ever known."

"And you've been around horses all your life, right?" Her first attempt to open her hand to Nell was met with skittishness, not by Nell but by Deanna, who pulled back before Nell could take the sugar. "Sorry, I'm a little nervous. This is as close as I've ever been to an animal this large. Will you show me how?"

He did. Placed four lumps in his own hand and gave the sugar to Nell, hand open and palm up. "It's easy," he said, handing another couple of cubes to Deanna. "Just relax and let Nell do the work."

Deanna smiled self-consciously, but still wasn't able to bring her hand all the way over to the mare's reach, so

Beau took hold of her hand and guided it to the horse. And held it as the horse very gently lifted her lips and took the sugar lumps.

"That's amazing," she whispered, as the last of the sugar disappeared from her hand. "I can see why you love them."

"First time I was on horse was with Brax," he said, slowly pulling his hand away from hers, glad to break the contact. "I was three, I think. Probably too young for most contemporary parental thinking, but he took care of me. Put me up on the saddle with him, and we only went around the yard. Didn't get past the driveway. But I felt so…free. And invincible, like I could do anything.

"Of course, Brax inspired that confidence in me as much as the horse did. But I was having a rough life and I think that's the first time I ever truly understood that things would work out for me, no matter what was scaring me, because my grandfather would take care of me."

"I'm sorry," she said, wiping the horse slobber from her hand on a rag Beau had handed her. "It's a rough way to grow up, but you were lucky in ways so many kids aren't. I've seen them abandoned, left to fend for themselves, raise younger siblings, go to work when they're supposed to be going to school. I think we take a roof over our heads and a meal on our tables for granted too often."

"True colors," Beau commented, stepping away from Nell's stable, satisfied she wouldn't foal in the next twenty-four hours and anxious to get away from the spell Deanna was casting over him. And she wasn't even trying, unlike Nancy, who'd come at him with every flirtatious trick in the book. But Deanna was so…so unassuming, so unaware of what her closeness could do to a man.

"I'm sorry?"

"Brax always taught me that a person's true colors reflected the deep-down self that comes out naturally, when they're not trying to impress or intimidate someone. Your true colors are nice. Very compassionate."

"I didn't have parents either. They were killed when I was five, and my aunt and uncle took me in and gave me that roof and food. So I was lucky, like you were with Brax, but Brax wanted you, whereas my aunt and uncle didn't want me.

"I was an obligation for them to fulfill and I think that's where my true colors, as you call them, came from—from my need to fix situations that others can't, or don't want to, fix. Growing up, my situation was never truly fixed. Anyway, why don't you finish up what you're doing here, and I'll go wash my hands then take a look at your office, see what's there, and check out what I'm going to be dealing with?"

"It's the white building out at the side of the house. Two exam rooms, one room for emergencies, and one for minor procedures. Waiting room, small office and a supply room. It was the original house here, and Brax turned it into his clinic when he built the house he's in now...for my grandmother. She refused to live in the place where he worked."

He fished a set of keys from his pocket and tossed them to Deanna. "Make yourself at home. Today's schedule is on the computer...my addition to the practice because Brax prefers keeping everything on paper. Password to log on is Alexander."

"Trying to sway me again?" she teased.

"Maybe a little."

"Well, between us, I prefer the computer to pen and paper, so that's a point in your favor."

With that, she exited. Didn't look back. Didn't even hesitate like she wanted to look back. Just kept walking. Deliberately. Confidently.

"There something to be said for a filly that's reserved, the way she is," Joey said, coming out of the stable office.

"I thought you were exercising the horses."

"Can't do that without a horse, and I didn't want to interrupt you to walk through the stalls, so I..."

Beau waved him off before he could finish, then spun around and strode out the door. Truth was, Joey was hitting close to home with his comments. Too close, and it was getting to Beau in ways it shouldn't. "Not going near it," he muttered with iron resolve as he headed for the house. "Nope, not going near it." Then he caught sight of Deanna entering the clinic and stopped and simply stared again. "Not going near it," he muttered again, but this time the resolve wasn't quite there.

So far, the afternoon was going well. Easy work, all things considered, even though she was feeling the effects of it in her lower back. It had been a long time since she'd done any kind of consistent physical nursing duty and, so far, she was loving it. Three patients had already passed through the exam room she'd commandeered for herself—simple cases but rewarding.

And she'd assisted Beau with one sweet little lady, aged eighty, who traditionally should have been home knitting or baking cookies but who'd inhaled a few too many paint fumes, turning her kitchen from pale blue to sunny yellow. She was fine, a little light-headed, which was what had brought her to the clinic, and together Deanna and Beau had given her a complete exam, just to be on the safe side. Deanna had an idea that Mrs. Eloise Hightower probably marched right back home afterwards to finish her decorating and sniff more paint.

"Doing OK?" Beau asked, passing Deanna in the hall.

"Actually, I'm enjoying this. Is the pace always this laid back?"

He chuckled. "This is a vacation. I've had days where they're lined up outside. And I've just taken on another house call this evening."

"But not on horseback, right? Because expecting me to do anything more with a horse than give it sugar lumps will subtract countless points from your side." A sly smile crossed her lips. "Keep that in mind, Doctor."

"I am, which is why we're going by SUV, like I promised. Don't want to evoke the wrath of the medical-practice arbiter, do I?"

"No wrath in me," she said as she disappeared into the supply closet to fetch forceps and all the other necessities required to extract one very large splinter from one little toe. "At least, not yet," she called over her shoulder, then laid her hand across her belly.

"He wants to get me…which would be *us*…up on a horse. Which I'm not going to do because, well, you know the reasons. But you should probably also be aware that your daddy's a little bit of a cowboy. Very handsome, too, in the rugged cowboy sense. He's not ready to admit what he wants though, and stand by it, because it conflicts with everything he's planned for himself. I think we all face that at one time or another, don't we?"

Deanna assessed for a baby bump, a little disappointed she wasn't feeling it yet, although she did feel life, and a deep sense of contentment. "You're not what I had planned either, but I'm happy." Happier now that she had a better sense of Beau. She liked him and, truthfully, she could go home tomorrow assured that this baby had the best coming from both parents.

But what about Beau? That was the question still plaguing her. Did he need to know about the baby? Did he even want to know? It had been her decision to come and find him but, as far as she knew, it was still his decision to be anonymous. Which made this tough.

He's living in a backwoods area called Sugar Creek, Tennessee, Miss Lambert. Working as the area doctor, I believe. Words from the private investigator she'd hired to find Braxton Alexander, after her lawyer had obtained the information.

Sure, she could have bought more information, probably paid for a life history, including all the nuances. But that had seemed wrong to her. Seemed too intrusive, especially as Braxton Alexander—Beau—had been an unidentified donor prior to her search.

We're sorry, Miss Lambert. Those records are confidential. We informed Mrs. Braxton of the paternity error because of the legalities involved. But we do not divulge identities, even in cases such as this.

Cases such as this...one lawyer and one private investigator later and here she was, walking through a perfect, tidy little doctor's office, getting ready to treat one of that error's patients.

And, admittedly, she was a little excited to do so. This was nice. All of it. The waiting area was small but cozy. Both exam rooms basic but stocked with everything a GP would need.

And Beau's office... She stepped inside and looked around on her way to yank the splinter. To the left was a wooden shelf filled with medical texts, some very old, some much newer. Two generations of learning, she guessed. Then there was the wall of certificates and diplomas. All bearing the name Braxton Beauregard Alexander. Some yellowed through the glass, some more pristine.

It was all Emily's baby's heritage, she thought as she ran her fingers over the glass covering Beau's medical diploma. It was also something that made her feel even more…conflicted. "I'll figure it out," she told the baby. "Give me time, and I promise I'll figure out what I'm supposed to do."

"It's really pretty simple," Beau said from the doorway.

She spun to face him, and he almost took her breath away he was so handsome. Something she'd already known, something she still wasn't getting over. "Wh-what?"

"The splinter. Sterilize it, give it tug if it's visible. If it's not, come get me and I'll make a cut…"

She shook her head. "I know how to remove a splinter. I was just wondering…" She looked back at all the diplomas of the two Braxton Alexanders, M.D. "It's easier if I don't know the people involved. I'm great at the impersonal decisions, but this is going to get personal, which means it's going to get complicated. I like Brax. And you. And it's like I'm the referee in the ring, ready to call the winner the one who comes out hitting the hardest. I'm not sure I can do it."

"Then don't. Either way, I promised you the surgery and exam room in Wyoming, and you'll get them."

"Without doing anything? Because so far I've treated sniffles and a scraped knee."

He smiled. "I need help, Deanna. But not at the cost of making you uncomfortable. So if you can't work here, I'll understand. And if you can't make suggestions about how Brax and I can work out our differences, I'll understand that as well."

"I want to," she said. And she did. But how could she be objective when every time she looked at Beau her breath caught and every time she thought about him she remembered that he was the father of Emily's baby? It was crazy.

Mixed up. Her pregnancy hormones weren't helping any by kicking in so often.

Yet she didn't want to leave. She knew what she needed to know, had seen what she needed to see, and still didn't to leave. "I'm not backing out of the agreement but just so you'll know, it's tough enough without you and Brax both trying to score points with me."

"Then I won't."

"As simple as that?" she asked.

"Simple as that." Rather than shaking hands with her when he extended his hand to hers, he held out a different set of forceps. "More precise than what you've got. Those belong to my grandfather, these belong to me. And that's not meant to sway you but to put the best surgical instrument in your hand."

"Good thing," she said, taking the instrument then scooting around him, practically holding her breath until she was well out of his sight.

"I've got to get over this," she said to the baby as she opened the door and greeted ten-year-old Tommy Dodson, whose foot was propped up on the exam table, his hand firmly in the clutch of a very nervous-looking mother.

The mother-child bond, she thought as she commenced prepping Tommy's toe. *It was a strong one.* And she looked forward to its tug. She also felt guilty, and that's the part that held her back. No matter how much she wanted this baby, she wanted Emily to have it even more. But that wasn't going to happen, was it?

"So tell me again how you got the splinter in your little toe. Something about climbing barefoot on the wood pile…?"

"It's crazy, trying to do so many things all at once," Deanna said, shrugging out of her white coat and hanging it on a hook on the back of the supply-room door, only to miss the hook and watch it slither to the floor.

"How do you keep up with it? Actually, how did your grandfather keep up with it? And he didn't use a computer for the paperwork." She'd seen five scheduled patients and three who'd just walked in. Plus two telephone consults. And Beau had doubled that during his afternoon.

"It's not meant to sway you but I keep up with it by avoiding the personal things that can get in the way. Like chitchat. I've found that if you ask Mrs. Milford how her cat's feeling today, or inquire about the status of Mr. Blanchard's latest carpentry undertaking, they'll tell you. At length. My grandfather did that, and I don't recall him ever seeming rushed. But it rushes me then I get grumpy, and all that shoots the day right out from under me. So, no chitchat."

Bending to pick up the lab coat, she felt a sharp jab in her back and gasped. "But he got through the day chitchatting and still delivered good medicine. So tell me how he did that, because I'd like to know." She grabbed the coat and straightened up, still fighting the kink that seemed to be becoming a permanent part of her back lately.

"You OK?" Beau asked, stepping up to her and grabbing hold as she finally made it back to fully upright.

"Nothing a nice long soak in a tub full of hot water wouldn't cure." Except, like horseback riding, that was off limits.

"Got a hot tub, if you're interested."

And it sounded so tempting, unfortunately… "Thanks, but there's one up at the cabin, if I want to use it." Which she wouldn't.

"Let me guess. You avoid hot tubs the way you do horseback rides?"

"What I avoid is wasting time, which is what we're

doing, especially since I'd like to get your house calls done before tomorrow morning."

"And dinner," he reminded her. "There's a little roadside stop halfway back from our last house call, and it over-looks, well…" He pointed out the window to the mountains. "More of that, only closer."

More of that was exactly what she needed. After such a short time here, she was already becoming addicted to the area—the mountains and trees, the lovely little stream that ran through the valley. Even the birds.

Except for the isolation, it was everything she wanted, not just for herself but for Emily's baby. It crossed her mind that if she did tell Beau this baby was his, he might want shared custody. Which meant Emily's baby would have all this, provided Beau stayed here. It was something to consider, one thing amongst so many.

"It sounds lovely," she said, heading to the door. "I'm going to run back to my cabin, change my shoes, splash some water on my face, and I'll be good to go. And maybe by the time we're on our way I'll have an idea of what to do about the patients who stop in without appointments, because you'd have been in the clinic for hours still if I hadn't been there to help."

"I think a few people came out just to see you. Normally I don't have so many minor casualties."

"But today you did, and that's the problem. What if I hadn't been here and you'd had that many people waiting, plus your house calls?

"And, Beau, you're using the computer, which is good, but the problem is it takes ten minutes to get a patient checked in and out, and you're doing that yourself. It's something a medical receptionist could do, if you had one." Which really did sway her to his side, she had to admit.

Beau held up his hands in mock surrender, smiled, and said nothing.

"OK, point taken. You're not going to comment. I get it."

"You're right. No comment. I'll just say go get ready for house calls, and I'll pick you up in thirty minutes. OK? And, Deanna…thanks. I'm not sure everything here is solvable, but I appreciate having someone who can see what frustrates me. And, no, that's not meant to sway you either. It's just a statement of fact and a hope that you can stay and figure out how to fix it because I know what I want, but I may be a little too involved to be as objective as I should be."

"You're not old-school medicine the way Brax is. Country GP has taken on a new definition, and Brax just hasn't come round to that. Which is fine because it works for him. But you're the new breed and that's good in so far as medical advances go, although I think in ways it's also a limiting on the personal level. The problem's easy enough to spot, although I'm not sure how easy it's going to be to fix. But medical solutions are what I do, so we'll see."

"Medical solutions, and making my day better. I'm probably going to thank you a thousand times over the next few weeks for doing this."

She smiled then waved him a quick goodbye and sprinted out the door. For what it was worth, he'd made her day better, too. Not just because he'd let her work in a different aspect of medicine than she was accustomed to but because he'd allowed her to see things she needed to see.

"I like your daddy," she said to the baby as she sped up the road to the cabin. "Now all we have to do is figure out if you'll ever have the opportunity to like him as well."

Late afternoon had taken on a cool edge, and Beau inhaled the pure mountain air deeply. It was good being home. He wasn't sure he could live up to the expectations of being the area's doctor but he didn't regret his temporary change of life.

He had big shoes to fill, though. Huge shoes, and most of the time people simply thought of him as the kid. Brax's grandson. Juvenile delinquent. So maybe his youthful reputation here hadn't been stellar, but Brax had handled it... had handled him. And he owed the old man more than he could repay.

He just wasn't sure, though, he could replace him. And that was the problem. If he stayed, new ways would have to replace the old. Deanna was seeing that, working directly in the middle of it. And he trusted her to make the right decisions.

But his grandfather was so resistant. Probably resentful that what had worked perfectly for him was being pushed aside. And there was no way in hell he would hurt his grandfather. That was the bottom line. In which case, maybe it would be easier to simply hire a doctor to come in and do the job at hand, and work with what was there, what was already established.

Someone else wouldn't be so...restless. And he was restless. Since his marriage and divorce, since his near—and fake—brush with fatherhood, it was like his world had turned upside down and had never quite righted itself. He wanted this life, he wanted his life back in New York. Wanted to be a country GP, wanted to be a surgeon. At the same time he didn't have a clue what he wanted.

So much indecision, all a year or more in the making, and he was no closer to figuring out what he was going to do now than he'd been a year ago when he'd come home.

And Deanna? He wasn't sure what he expected from her. Maybe someone who would support some tough changes that would have to happen if he stayed. Or support his decision to leave, if that's what it came to.

Maybe, though, she was a distraction. Something to take his mind off the things he didn't want to think about.

Whatever the case, Brax was on his way to town for the evening, and as he helped his grandfather out to the pick-up truck, Beau's gaze inadvertently went up to the ridge where Deanna's cabin loomed over the back acreage. Rather than looking away, he let himself stare for a moment—stare and wonder about the woman up there. She wasn't here to do what she claimed. He knew that and he believed she knew he knew. For now the illusion would stand, but he was curious.

"I can see why you'd enjoy coming out here to make house calls," Deanna said. She was seated next to Beau in his four-wheel-drive SUV, glad they were in something woods-worthy. "I'm not a deep-woods kind of a girl, but this is lovely."

Trees were so dense that the fading daylight trickled in only in ribbons. The undergrowth of rhododendrons with their lush purple flowers grew expansively under the thick green canopy. And there was a richness to the air that she'd never known could exist. These were the areas she cared about in her work yet they were areas she rarely ever saw, and being out in the thick of it made her feel very limited by her academic focus.

Deanna was gaining, first hand, a totally new understanding of what medical life in these isolated areas was like, and it made her wonder how much she was missing, both professionally and personally.

"It's a different way of life," Beau said. "When I was a kid, I couldn't wait to get out of here. But now it's nice to be back. Makes me realize just how hectic it is in the city."

"You thrive on hectic, though, don't you?"

"I thrive on work. If it's hectic, that's fine because it keeps me away from…"

"A personal life?" she ventured.

"I excel in medicine, but I don't excel in the personal. When I was a kid I was…let's call it antisocial. Found a certain confidence in it, I think."

"Yes, you did mention you were a troublemaker."

He chuckled. "I like to think of it as being a result of my father, but the reality is I was just a brat. That was my nature. But Brax taught me how to turn that into hard work, and showed me how hard work paid off. It was a better way."

"Then being at odds with him the way you are now makes you feel, what? Guilty?"

"Very perceptive, Nurse Lambert."

"Doesn't take a lot of perception to see it. But what I also see is two very stubborn men who are fighting *not* to meet in the middle." Would that stubbornness pass along to the baby?

"I've practiced medicine outside Sugar Creek, he hasn't."

"Which makes you right…in your opinion."

"Which makes me right as far as the way I want to work here. If I stay."

"So what it boils down to is your way or you leave. And you're hoping that my presence, and my professional recommendations, will substantiate your way." Yes, *very* stubborn. But it was laced with determination and dedication, and she liked that quality in him. She hoped that, more than the stubbornness, would carry through to the baby.

"When you put it that way, it sounds pretty confrontational, doesn't it?" He slowed the SUV where the road turned into a barely passable path, then killed the engine.

"Oh, and from here we walk. But it's only about a quarter-mile."

"Seriously, people live out here? How do they get in and out?"

"Back road. It's shorter, and steeper, and hell on a vehicle's suspension, so I prefer the longer, slower, easier road. And it's a pleasant walk, by the way."

"It had better be," she grumbled good-naturedly, grabbing her medical bag then sliding down to the ground. "Because this wasn't in my job description." Although, truth be told, she was looking forward to the hike. Working on her feet all day had only made her crave more and, for someone who spent a good part of her days at a computer, this was just what she and the baby needed.

"And, yes, it does sound confrontational. But sometimes we have to draw our line in the sand and stick to it, don't we? Even if the person on the other side is someone you love. Makes life interesting, I think."

"You're very cagey," he said, taking her medical kit and strapping it onto the backpack he'd slung over his shoulder. "And I have an idea if Brax had gotten to you first, you'd be wholeheartedly on his side."

"I don't take sides in my work. I do have opinions…objective opinions I offer the people who need my ideas. And subjective opinions, which I keep to myself. But it's always about what's best for the medical community as a whole."

"But you favor Brax." Statement, not question.

"I favor whatever works best for Sugar Creek. I haven't seen enough yet to decide what I think it is. But I'll warn you it's going to involve compromises on both sides. Experience has taught me the best solution always does."

He laughed. "Like I said, cagey."

"Been called worse," she said, taking hold of the hand he extended her at the trail head and stepping lightly over the trunk of a fallen tree on which countless people had carved initials. She studied it for a moment. Smiled. Thought about all the people who'd hiked this trail before. Wondered about their names.

"Are your initials there?" she asked, once they cleared the spot and he'd let go of her.

"Nope. You carve your initials and that's…permanence. Not sure I'm ready for that yet."

"Does that have to do with your bad marriage?" she asked, fully realizing it was none of her business. But she wanted to take the liberty anyway, to find out more about this man. "Because the walk down that aisle means permanence, and you took that walk."

"In a weak moment. She was pretty."

"So beauty turned your head, but couldn't keep it turned?"

"Beauty married me for my money, as it turned out."

"And broke your heart?"

"Not that so much as embarrassed the hell out of me. Look out for that root," he warned, reaching out to take her hand again.

She was glad to hold onto him, and it wasn't because of the trail. She liked his touch. Soft hands, but strong. Protective. Something she'd never really had in her life. "This is the first of six house calls?" she asked, stepping a little closer to him.

"The others aren't so isolated. Diabetes check, blood-pressure check, short procedures. Thought we'd get the most interesting case, and longest visit, out of the way first."

"Sounds like you look forward to this part of your grandfather's practice."

"Do I detect that you might be trying to trap me into some kind of confession?"

She laughed. "Just trying to point out that you like parts of his practice. That's all."

"What I like is simplicity in a system that works for me. That's the way I was in New York, and it's the way I am here. It's part of who I am. It became a bigger part, I think, after my marriage ended and I was trying to put back the pieces of me she'd taken away." He turned to look at her. "Have you ever been married?"

"No."

"Ever come close?"

"Not really. Haven't ever met someone I'd want to be that serious with."

"Maybe that's smart. Live your life for yourself, keep any involvement at arm's length. Because once you open that door and let it in..." He shrugged. Cringed. "Sometimes you can't stop the momentum. If it's what you want, that's fine. But if it's not, you're in more trouble than you ever knew could happen, and there's not always an easy way out of it."

"So, you're anti-marriage? Anti-relationship? Which one?"

"Neither, and both. I did it so badly the first time I'm not sure I'd trust myself to try it again."

"Which is why you need help with the decision on whether to stay here or go back to New York? You choose badly. Is that it?" He was insightful into his own process, but she wasn't thrilled about his conclusions because if she did decide to tell him about his baby, she wasn't sure how he'd take the news. There were moments when she thought he'd be thrilled, but now, hearing all this, she doubted he'd even want to know.

And his view on relationships as a whole was pretty discouraging. Maybe that's what bothered her most.

"I made a bad choice once and I'm trying to stop myself from doing it again."

"But you can't equate marriage to a medical practice."

"What I can equate, though, is blindness to blindness. I was blinded by Nancy. And I'm also blinded by my own likes and especially dislikes as a doctor. They're not that different from each other. I see what I want to see and put on blinkers to the rest. That's what I'm trying to overcome right now. With your help."

"With my help." She admired his openness. In her experience, most people either wouldn't admit their weaknesses or couldn't see them. Beau was extraordinary in this, though, and it was another nice trait she hoped would be passed to the baby. It also made her wish Beau could be the one to actually teach or nurture that strength in his child.

In fact, she wished for it so much she could almost picture Beau walking through these very woods hand in hand with a toddler, teaching him or her about life in general. Pointing out trees and birds and flowers. Stopping to examine a shiny rock or look at an ant scurrying its way home to its colony. It was such a nice image, it elicited a sigh from her.

"Tired?" he asked.

"A little bit. But I'm also wondering what's going to be interesting about this first house call."

Beau chuckled. "You'll see, in about five minutes."

And she did. After five minutes of idle chitchat and watching out for other tree roots and rocks hidden by vegetation, they came to a little cottage. A well-kept cottage, actually. It looked freshly painted. White. With green shutters. And totally out of place here, in the middle of the woods. No one around for miles. "So, who's our patient?"

"Arthur Jeremiah Handler."

"*The* Arthur Jeremiah Handler?" His paintings were legendary. And very, very expensive, as he only did one or two a year.

"He found this place when he was scouting a location to paint, and that was thirty-five years ago. I remember Brax bringing me up here, and it always seemed like such an adventure. Sometimes we'd camp out in Arthur's front yard for a night, build a huge bonfire, cook our dinner, sleep in a tent. Although I think Brax usually sneaked out after I went to sleep and stayed in Arthur's guest room."

"Then he's a recluse?"

"Not at all. He just likes separation when he's painting. When he's not painting, he lives in Paris."

"So I take it he's painting."

Beau nodded as he knocked on the door. "Chronic diabetes, by the way. He maintains it well here, but when he's in Paris…"

"When I'm in Paris the magnificent pastries are my comeuppance," Arthur Jeremiah Handler said, opening the door to them. "Beau, thanks for coming. Have you gotten yourself married again?" Arthur asked, first giving Deanna a very deliberate head-to-toe appraisal then pulling her into his ample embrace.

"Because this one is much better than the last one. Prettier. More intelligence in her eyes. Doesn't radiate distrust and manipulation the way your Nancy did."

"Not married," Deanne managed to squeeze out while still enfolded in his meaty arms. "Just working as his nurse."

"A nurse?" Arthur bellowed. He finally loosened his hug. "How's Brax handling that? Not good, I imagine."

"No, not good," Beau said, stepping inside then taking hold of Deanna's hand and pulling her well past Arthur. "And this is Deanna Lambert, by the way. She's a consul-

tant for medical practices, and she's agreed to help me for
the next month."

"Nice to meet you," Deanna said, looking around at the
cottage. It was lush. Huge leather furniture. Antique brass
figures everywhere. Rich-colored paintings she took to be
Arthur's own work. All of it a man's world.

"Not as nice as it is to meet you," Arthur replied, wig-
gling very bushy white eyebrows at her. "Rare beauty such
as yours is welcome in this home any time it presents itself on my doorstep."

"Knock off the charm, Arthur. Deanna's all business.
Probably rather stick you with a lancet than listen to you."

She liked the fondness between the two men. Arthur,
who was probably Brax's age, looked like Santa Claus,
with a round belly and a white beard. And the most amazing, astute eyes. So much so they almost scared her. But he
was an artist so he saw the world through an artist's eyes.
Still, the way he was staring at her right now...

"If you insist on using the lancet, my dear, you may
have any finger I possess," he said, holding out his right
hand and turning it palm up for her. "In fact, you may have
all of them, if you wish. But before you make me bleed, I
think it's fair to warn you that I have indulged on the finest Paris has to offer and my test results here will reflect
that I haven't eaten as wisely as I should."

"An A1C blood test will tell us everything we need to
know about your eating, Mr. Handler," she said, pulling
an alcohol swab from her kit, ripping it open then cleaning the tip of his index finger. "Unfortunately, I'm not prepared to do that kind of a blood draw here, so I may have
to schedule you into the clinic in the very near future."

Pulling the lancet device from her kit, she anchored a
fresh lancet in it then warned him, "Little stick." Said after

the stick, actually. She waited five seconds for the results then said, "Normal."

"Of course it's normal. I'm always a good boy when I'm in Sugar Creek. By the way, Beau, does your nurse know I avoid doctors' offices?" Arthur asked. "Absolutely abhor those dismal little places. They're for sick people who have infectious coughs and other disgusting symptoms."

Beau chuckled. "But Deanna is pretty formidable, Arthur. If she schedules you an appointment, I wouldn't go up against her if I were you.

Arthur turned to regard Deanna and opened his mouth to protest, but she beat him to it. "A full panel of blood tests, Mr. Handler. And a routine EKG as well to rule out any heart problems that might result from those Paris indulgences. Things that can't be done on a house call. I have an opening for you next Monday. First thing in the afternoon, say, one o'clock. Shouldn't take more than an hour. So, may I count on you being there?"

"Miserable things those damned office appointments," he grumbled. "Besides, Brax and young Beau do a respectable job here so why drag me out for something I don't need?"

"But I've told you it was time you came in and had a proper physical," Beau interjected.

"To no avail, young man." He turned a pointed glance at Deanna. "And young woman. Because I will not cross the threshold to your clinic. Not next Monday. Not any Monday."

"And you thought Brax was stubborn," Beau commented to Deanna.

"Your grandfather is a mere amateur," Arthur said, "but I have perfected stubbornness to an art form."

"So, are you and your stubbornness ready for an exam, Arthur?" Beau asked.

"By an exam you mean…"

"An exam." Beau grinned. "Everything I can do on a house call."

"Then I'm going to have to ask your nurse to please go fix us a pot of tea because there are parts of myself I've never exposed to a woman, and never intend on exposing to a woman. And I'm not being a chauvinist, Miss Lambert. I'm merely trying to cling to the last shred of dignity a man my age has."

She liked him. Liked his manners, his charm. Especially liked his wit. "With cream, sugar, lemon?"

"Civilized, my dear. Cream, light sugar. Oh, and I've just pulled some fresh bread from the oven…yes, I do bake. It's a pity some woman didn't latch onto me in my prime.

"Anyway, please help yourself to whatever you want. Jam is in the fridge, along with an assortment of fresh vegetables and fruits. I'm sure a woman in your condition could use a healthy snack after the ordeal Beau has put you through working with him."

"My condition?" she sputtered, not sure what he meant.

"With child, of course."

"But…" No, she wouldn't deny it. In fact, back home nothing about her pregnancy had been a secret. But here, in front of Beau… "I mean…"

"It's in your glow, my dear. I've painted dozens of ladies with the same glow. Did a portrait series of the various stages of pregnancy so I recognize it the instant I see it."

"You didn't tell me," Beau murmured, clearly shocked.

"You're not my doctor. And I'm barely started." As if to prove her point, she ran her hand over her perfectly flat belly, only…was it larger today than it had been yesterday? Or was her imagination getting the better of her? "And healthy. Capable of fixing a pot of tea, too," she said, then scooted into the kitchen and leaned heavily against the first available wall she could find.

Now what? Stay here and keep on doing what she was doing? Or leave, convinced that Beau was a good man?

And still wonder why he'd become a donor. That was the biggest question that remained. By all observations, he wasn't social, didn't want involvement. Yet agreeing to father an anonymous child somewhere was about as social and involved as it got without true involvement. She didn't understand it. The thing was, even if she knew all the nuances, all the details, it wouldn't make a difference. She was carrying his baby, and she was going to raise it. Nothing about that would change.

Yet she didn't want to leave. Not yet. "So we're right back to the place where I don't know what to do," she whispered to the baby. Then shut her eyes. Tried to wipe everything from her mind but the life inside her. Which, in her mind's eye, right now was a little boy who looked just like his daddy.

"You OK?" Beau asked from the kitchen doorway.

"Where's Arthur?"

"Getting ready to be examined. So, how far along are you?"

"Nine weeks. Sailing through it like a champ."

"And keeping it a secret?" he asked.

She shook her head. "Not really. Just didn't have too many opportunities to insert it into our conversations." She shrugged. "No big deal."

"What about the father? Is it a big deal to him?"

"Nope. He made a one-time deposit in the sperm bank, I benefitted. Good for him, I suppose. Wonderful for me."

Beau raised questioning eyebrows. "But you don't seem happy."

"Quite the contrary. There's nothing I want to do more

than bring this baby into the world and be the best mom I can possibly be."

"Then smile when you say that, Deanna, because I'm not convinced."

"You don't have to be," she said, stepping away from the wall and heading to the old-fashioned gas stove to fetch the tea kettle. "For what it's worth, though, I wanted to do this. From the very first moment Em...I thought about it, it's all I wanted. So if you're not seeing happiness, it's because you're not looking. Arthur saw it right off. You know, that pregnancy glow. And I'm sure, by now, he's ready to get your poking and prodding over with."

He studied her for a moment then nodded. "And for what it's worth, good decision about the horseback riding. I just wonder why you didn't tell me that was the reason." Then he left the kitchen.

"You didn't know?" Arthur asked. "From the way you look at her...I thought the baby might be yours. Miss Lambert is a far sight better than what you ended up with the first time."

"I've only known her a couple of days. And she's *only* my consultant. That's all."

"With that look I saw in your eyes, Beau, I think you've known her a lifetime. Or wanted to know her." He grinned. "Now, tell me what you want me to do because I'd like to get this whole mess over with and go have tea with that lovely *consultant* of yours."

Beau snapped on a glove. "Guess what comes next," he said.

He'd thought she was reserved, and now he knew why. Still, she didn't seem happy enough. Especially for someone who'd made the choice to bring a baby into the world on her own. It was a tough decision but an exciting one. In Deanna, though, he saw confusion where he should have been seeing joy. There was something else, he decided. But he couldn't imagine what. More than that, he couldn't imagine why he cared. He did, though. He cared, and he didn't want to explore the reasons why. In fact, he didn't even want to think that there might *be* a reason.

CHAPTER FIVE

"I LIKE YOUR FRIEND," Deanna said. She was settling into a chair at an outside table that sat, quite literally, over the mountain stream running directly beneath the little restaurant where they were about to dine. It was a cozy place, its ambience more like an elevated patio, enclosed by screens rather than walls, with casual outdoor furniture and low lighting in the form of muted Japanese lanterns. While it wasn't elegant, and in the full light of day might have looked a bit tacky, Beau's choice was a comfortable one. And tonight all she wanted was comfort.

It had turned into a very long day for her. And a hard one as well, since the physicality of the day had finally caught up to her.

Still now, at day's end, she was beginning to realize how much she missed real nursing duties, the kind where you spent your day with people, not research, phones and computers. "He's quite charming. Very direct."

"Arthur? He was my port in the storm several times when I was growing up. You know, that adult figure with a voice of reason who just seemed to understand you better than your parents did. Or, in my case, Brax. That's what I thought, anyway. And you're right. He is very direct."

"I saw one of his paintings once, years ago, in a museum. And I thought he must be a serene man, the way he captured the essence of the mountainscape. I mean, how many people have painted mountains and trees and done so adequately but unremarkably? Yet in that painting it was like I was there, and I could feel that same peacefulness he must have felt when he was painting it.

"In fact, that painting is what inspired me into rural nursing research. When I discovered that places like he painted struggled for the medical care most people are accustomed to…I guess it bothered me that just off the edge of the canvas there were hard realities to deal with.

"Anyway, here I am, and I just fixed him a pot of tea, Beau! The man makes a difference in the world, and I fixed him a pot of tea."

She was perplexed, though, why someone like A. J. Handler would isolate himself the way he did. He belonged to the world, and the world was a better place when he was in it and not hiding out in a secluded mountain cabin.

"I have an idea you could stop by and fix him a pot of tea any time you wanted. He loves having visitors. And I noticed that he said he *might* stop by the office for an exam. That's the one thing I never expected from him."

"He's an old sweetie. Just needs a little nudging, that's all. But why does he live so far away from everything? Especially if he loves having people stop by?"

"I don't believe he thinks he's far from everything. In fact, I'm pretty sure Arthur believes he's living in the center of his universe. Guess it depends on your perspective, doesn't it?"

"And on what makes you happy." She glanced at the menu, ordered a dinner-sized salad and green tea, along with a basket of home-made rolls, then shut her eyes for a moment to concentrate on the sound of the stream coming in through the screened walls. So peaceful, so relaxing…it almost made her forget New York for a moment. Almost made her forget she really didn't belong here.

"Sometimes happy is hard to figure out," Beau said, after his order for mountain trout was placed. "When I was a kid, happy was the new bicycle I wanted more than anything I'd ever wanted in my entire life. I worked hard for it, took on extra chores, saved my money and on the day I went to buy it, there was another bike in the shop, a lot nicer, and a lot more expensive.

"It would have been weeks before I could afford it, so I bought the one I'd originally had my heart set on but I was never happy with it. Essentially, what made me happy one moment turned into a reminder of what I wasn't happy with for a long time afterwards."

"I learned early on that you're responsible for your own happiness. It's what you create for yourself, or nurture in yourself."

"Then that would preclude finding happiness in someone else, or loving someone who makes you happy."

"You said you were divorced, so do you still believe in that?" she asked, as she picked up the iced tea the server had just brought over. "I mean, I think anybody who marries expects to find happiness, but you went through it and got out. And look at you now. You're trying to find some kind of life right here, which I suppose could be translated into happiness. But it doesn't include someone else. It's what you're trying to create for yourself, and I'm not sure it was in your plan when you married…"

"Nancy. Her name is Nancy. And, no, what I'm going through right now wasn't part of *that* plan. But I'd hate to go through life believing that the only person who can make me happy is me. That my happiness is dependent only on something of my creation."

He was an optimist, she decided. A believer in things

greater than himself. She liked that, actually. She didn't have the same kind of optimistic outlook herself, but she liked it that the baby's father had that in him.

"I'm not saying that happiness can't happen *because of* somebody else, or even *with* somebody else." She was certainly happy because of the baby. "But you shouldn't depend on it because if you sit around and wait for it to happen, you might miss out on something good."

"Like being a mother?"

"Like being a mother," she said, almost reverently. "But I wasn't supposed to be this baby's mother. It was never my intention to have a baby for myself."

"Then you're…"

"Carrying this baby for my cousin. Her embryo, actually. But she died, and I wasn't left with many options. There was a mix-up. Somehow sperm samples got switched, and Emily's baby…the baby I'm carrying didn't belong to her husband. After she died, he signed all the choices over to me and walked away…"

Beau tilted his head with concern.

"I was deriving my happiness from helping her find hers. But things change. Certainly my direction did, yet I'm still creating my own happiness by knowing that I'm bringing Emily's baby into the world the way she wanted, and I'll be the best possible mother I can be."

"But happiness doesn't have to be something you create. It should be something you simply have. Something that flows in and out naturally. I wanted to be happy in my marriage. I expected to be, and it didn't work out. But I never, once, thought that I had to somehow build or create that happiness. It should have come as part of having everything I wanted. The fact that it didn't is unfortunate, but it doesn't take away from my basic faith that when the pieces of your life fall into the right place, happiness is what happens."

"Or should happen."

He smiled. "Be patient with yourself. Maybe you haven't found it yet, but that doesn't mean you won't. Your baby is where you start, I think."

"Not my baby," she said, almost to herself. Because it wasn't. It was Beau's baby, and Emily's. And maybe that's what washed the melancholy mood over her, thinking that her cousin had created something with Beau—that happiness—she never would. "Anyway, enough of that. I'm really tired, and as soon as we've eaten, I'd like to go back to my cabin, because I've got another couple of hours of research ahead of me tonight."

"What you've got ahead of you is resting. As in going to bed. Or reading a romance novel or listening to whatever kind of music you like to listen to."

"Classical."

"Then classical it is, because your working day is over. Doctor's orders, and if he as to, Doctor's going to hang around for a while to make sure you do what you're supposed to. Oh, and while we're on the subject, I think we'll skip the house calls now that I know—"

She thrust out her hand to stop him. "I know my limits, Beau. I appreciate your concern but, please, let me be the one to tell you when I'm not able to make a house call. OK?"

He reached over and took hold of her hand. "I'm sorry for your loss, Deanna. In everything we were talking about, I think that aspect got misplaced. But you must have loved her very much to want to carry her child, and I'm sorry she died."

"So am I," she whispered, batting back a sudden tear. "I try not to think about it because it's not good for the baby. But she was my best friend. My only friend. And sometimes I feel so…" She shook her head. "Hormones flipping over, making me weepy. Sorry."

"'Tis a far nobler thing…"

She sniffed away the last of her tears and smiled. "I appreciate the compliment, but taking care of someone you love isn't noble. It's what life's supposed to be about. You take care of Brax, I take care of Emily's baby. It's the way the universe is suppose to work."

"Are you going to be OK? I don't want to take you back to the cabin and leave you there alone. Let's just say hormonal, weepy, pregnant women should have a shoulder to cry on. That's the way the universe is supposed to work, too."

"You're kind," she said. "But the problem with pregnancy is you never know what's going to make you cry or when it's going to happen. So for me to have your shoulder, you'd have to stay with me twenty-four hours a day."

"I've stayed in worse places," he said.

Why did he have to be so nice? Why did he have to be the kind of man it would be so easy to fall in love with? The kind of man she'd fall in love with if she were the falling kind? "Is that a compliment?"

"I'm not sure you'd be easy with a personal compliment, would you?"

Before she had a chance to answer, the server brought their dinners to the table. Her salad, his mountain trout. As soon as the plates were on the table, Beau switched them. Took the salad himself, and moved the plate with broiled trout, fresh asparagus and brown rice in front of her. "No arguments," he warned. "Your baby needs more than lettuce and tomatoes after the day you've given him, or her."

"I'm too tired to eat," she protested.

"Tell that to your baby, who's probably craving protein."

"The baby's two months along," she said, grabbing back her salad. "And I'm on good prenatal vitamins for nights like this when I don't eat as well as I should. But thanks for fussing. I haven't had anyone to support me in this pregnancy, and it's nice to think someone cares."

"Someone does care."

"Why, Beau? We've known each other a few days, so why would you care? You're not my doctor, not even my friend, really. So I don't understand it."

Rather than answering, Beau forked up a bite of flaky fish and reached across the table with it. Headed directly for her lips. "Open up," he said. "One bite, and I'll tell you why I care."

She did have to admit the fish smelled divine. And it tasted as good as it smelled as it passed between her lips. Savoring the moment, the food, the pure sensual feel of being fed by him, she lingered as long as she could before she had to swallow, almost regretting that the moment had ended. Another place, another time, it could have been so romantic... "OK, tell me."

"I like you."

"That's it? You like me?"

He forked up another bite of fish and held it out for her. "One more bite and I'll tell you."

It was all she could do to keep from melting under the table as the second bite passed her lips and she watched his hand slip back over to his side of the table and break off yet another piece of fish. Meaning another bite... "Two bites down, now tell me."

"You're smart. You're efficient. Most of all you're independent, which, since my divorce, I value more than almost anything else in a woman."

Well, not the compliments she would have liked, but

they were honest. And this wasn't a romantic scenario after all.

A sly grin slid across his face. "Oh, and you're easy on the eye."

Now, that pleased her. "Did you forget that I'm pregnant?"

He held up the third bite and she took it. When she'd finished, he said, "Pregnant is beautiful. Nancy, when she was thinking about getting pregnant, was having fits about gaining the weight, getting swollen ankles, looking frumpy. She was willing to put up with it to get my money, but she wouldn't have been pleasant to live with."

"Before I say anything, no more bites, please. I really do want to eat my salad, and I've already eaten too much of your meal."

"You sure?"

She smiled. "Sure. And I do worry about the weight gain and the swollen ankles, but not in terms of how I'll look so much as my overall condition. I have to stay healthy for this baby. But as far as looking frumpy...who cares?"

"Which gets back to my original statement. I like you, and that's just another of the reasons why."

"But you didn't know that about me until just now."

"It's an assumption I could make, though. One, among many."

"So now you're making assumptions about me?"

"A few."

She stabbed a cherry tomato with her fork and poised it halfway across the table, feeling bolder than she'd ever felt before. "So, can I tempt you with my tomato, Doctor? You tell me your assumption, I'll give you my tomato."

"Sounds like a bribe to me," he said, his voice a little rougher than usual.

"Maybe it is, maybe it's just a simple offer of salad. But only if you tell me one of those assumptions."

"You're practical."

"Not enough to get my tomato."

"Caring."

"That should be a given considering I'm a nurse."

"But you're a nurse researcher, which could lead me to a different direction with my assumptions."

"Such as?"

"People frighten you in the personal sense. Or, you don't understand them. Or you're afraid they'll hurt you."

This was going much deeper than she wanted it to, because he was right about all of it. And she didn't know what kind of answer to give him and still keep the distance she wanted. But as it turned out, she didn't have to answer him because he plunged ahead. "And you're a good kisser?"

"A good kisser?" she sputtered.

He nodded. "Beautiful lips. Nice and full. They look very soft. And you don't wear lipstick... I hate lipstick. Prefer the natural look. Which leads me to the assumption that you're a good kisser." With that, he took the fork from her hand, ate the tomato, then handed her back an empty fork. "Am I right?"

"Don't know," she said, spearing a cucumber slice for herself. "Don't rightly recall that anyone's ever critiqued my kissing."

"Pity," he said. "I'd like to read the review. Anyway, I deserve another cherry tomato for baring practically my entire soul to you."

"Your soul?"

"Well, maybe not my soul but my fondest wish."

"Which is?"

"Nancy wore hideous, fire-engine red lipstick. All the time. Day, night, to bed. My fondest wish is that if I ever do get involved again, I want the lady in question to have natural lips. Like yours." With that, he turned his attention to his dinner and she dove right into hers, and the conversation went medical for the rest of the evening.

Which was for the best, she decided a little later as she entered her cabin and he went to do the gentlemanly thing by putting on a pot of tea. Yes, it was definitely for the best they stay on safe territory because, given the chance, and one more cherry tomato or bite of mountain trout, she might have shown him what it felt like to be kissed *au naturel*.

CHAPTER SIX

"Part of me really believes he should know," Deanna whispered to the baby. "But only if he wants to, and that's the problem. I don't know what he wants. So we just do what we're already doing, and keep taking it one day at a time."

She went into the great room, where she turned on the large-screen TV, popped on an old Kathryn Hepburn movie she'd found in the cabin's collection, settled down onto the sofa, hoping it would agree with the growing ache in her lower back, and promptly started relaxing to the raspy-voiced Kathryn having her way with her on-screen hero.

"I'm settled in," she called to Beau. "Doing what the doctor ordered."

"Not working on a report, are you? Or doing some research? Hiding it under the covers so you won't get caught?"

She laughed. "No. I'm getting ready to relax with a movie."

"And the world didn't come to an end because you're taking the rest of the evening off, did it?"

It unnerved her how well he knew her. Especially in such a short time. Was she that transparent? Could he see her confusion, or the intent on her face every time he looked at her? "I'm really not that obsessed."

"Yes, you are," he shouted over the screech of the tea kettle's whistle. "And stubborn, too. Sort of like the pot calling the kettle black when you call me stubborn."

This was nice, she had to admit. Cozy on the couch, Beau standing watch for a little while. And Hepburn... Hepburn was always strong, the way Deanna wanted to always be strong. "The way I'm going to teach you to be strong," she said to the baby, as she pulled a blanket from the back of the sofa down over her.

"But you're going to have real role models in your life, not images on screens the way I did. Me, maybe even your da..." On a sigh, her day drifted away for a little while, even before her tea had completely steeped.

Beau set the tea aside and simply stood in the doorway, watching her. She slept with a smile on her face. He'd never really seen that before. He'd read about it in books, seen it portrayed in movies, but had never witnessed it. But yes, Deanna slept with a smile on her face. Beautiful face, he thought. Not angelic. Not even soft. Beautiful in character and determination. Especially beautiful in strength. A face he could get used to looking at, though.

Exhausted, Beau slumped down into the chair across from her and kicked off his boots. He promised himself he'd rest for five minutes, then drag himself out and go home. So, propping his feet up on a footstool, he leaned back, cupped his hands behind his head, and simply existed there, listening to the gentle in and out of Deanna's breathing, wondering about the way she faced the world.

There wasn't really a way to define it. Maybe head on. Or combatively. Yet there were these moments, these off-guard moments, when he'd see such vulnerability in her eyes. And sadness. Maybe that's what pulled him in the most. And now he understood why. She was having someone else's baby, a very altruistic thing to do. Also something that had turned out so tragically.

It couldn't be easy, having everything change like that. Like the way everything had changed in his life. *How do you expect me to get pregnant when you're never home? It's not like that window of opportunity is open every day of every week of every month, Beau.* OK, so Nancy had made him feel guilty. But in his defense those had been busy days, fighting for his place in the hospital hierarchy, being saddled with more responsibility than someone in his upwardly mobile position needed.

Then life had changed for him as well. And with him, like it was with Deanna, it could never change back. But it could get more complicated, he thought as he watched her sleep.

This was complicated, sitting here, watching her sleep. It's because she's pregnant, he tried to convince himself. That's all. It was the right thing to do, trying to help her.

"Beau?"

He resisted opening his eyes. His five minutes weren't up yet and he was too tired to move.

"Beau, it's seven o'clock."

Couldn't be. He hadn't gone home yet.

"I've made a pot of coffee."

Yes, he could smell it. "Five minutes," he protested, slowly becoming aware that he'd spent the entire night in the chair.

"Brax called and…"

Instantly alert, Beau opened his eyes and pushed himself from slumped to straight up. "Brax? Is he OK?"

Deanna laid a reassuring hand on his shoulder. "He's fine. Just wondering where you were. I told him you'd stayed over and that you were sleeping like a baby. He wanted you to know that Nell's on the verge of giving birth. Your pregnant horse, right?"

Nodding, Beau ran his fingers through his hair and forced himself to wake up. "One of my horses. Ran a few races, won, then pulled up lame. So we bred her with another champ, hoping to produce a champion."

"It sounds so clinical."

"It *is* clinical. I found what I thought would be a good genetic match for her, bought the frozen semen…"

He looked up, saw that her face had gone ashen. "What?" he asked, pushing himself out of the chair. "What's wrong?

"Nothing. Nothing's wrong. I just need to…take a shower…" She swallowed hard. Looked up at him. "Why wouldn't you have simply put her out in a pasture with one of your stallions and let nature take its course?"

"Because nature's course in the case of my two stallions wasn't good enough. If the best was out there to be had, that's what I wanted. Because…" He shrugged. "Because I wanted to produce championship offspring. Or, at least, take my best shot at producing a champ. It's done all the time, Deanna. People want—"

"Champions," she said.

"What just happened?" he asked, stepping forward, only to have her step back. "You went from friendly to…I guess the best way to describe it would be stricken."

"Backache. Comes and goes."

She wasn't telling the truth. It was obvious. In fact, the expression on her face was a dead giveaway when she was trying to be evasive. It had all started when he'd mentioned inseminating his horse, which had probably reminded her of… Damn, he was stupid!

"Look, I'm sorry. I know it sounded like a cold, calculating thing, having my horse inseminated, but in the animal world it's a big business."

"In the people world, too. Choose a pretty face from a book, check their IQ, their profession, their background. What's not big business about that?"

Hormonal swing? Maybe he'd just touched a raw nerve. The problem was, with Deanna he wasn't sure how to un-touch it. "It was a choice, Deanna. You, Emily and her husband…a choice from your heart to help them. That's not big business. In fact, it's about as personal as it gets."

"It's just too close," she said, shrugging. "Especially when I'm still not used to…to any of it."

"For what it's worth, you're going to make a sensational mother." He reached for his boots and regretted having to put them on, but he was already an hour late starting his day and he did want to get down to Nell to see how the birthing was progressing.

"I see it in you, Deanna. And that's not the doctor ob-serving the nurse but me observing you. Even if your sit-uation isn't what you might have chosen for yourself, that baby you're carrying is one lucky little kid to be getting you."

She walked over to the rear window and looked out at Brax's pasture for a moment. Then drew in a deep breath and let it out.

"I'm not a nurturer the way you're supposed to be when you have children, Beau. I rely on judgement, knowledge and skill, but I don't have that natural instinct good moth-ers have. For this baby, there are things I know I have to do—eat properly, get good rest, avoid certain activities.

"But that's all knowledge from a book, not knowledge from inside me. And I think getting myself so deeply en-trenched in Sugar Creek almost from the moment I arrived is a distraction I probably, subconsciously, want because it puts off the inevitable."

"Which is?"

"Wondering if I can be a good mother to this baby." She swiped at tears she didn't want to shed, especially so early in the day. "It's all I worry about now, and I'm sure some of this is a hormonal swing. That, plus my back hurts and I'm not even…" She gestured a big belly.

"I can't help you with the hormonal swings, and other than telling you I think you're going to be a fantastic mother there's nothing I can do about that. But I can do something for your back, if you let me." he said. Standing, he walked over to the window, stood behind her, but kept his distance. "You have to be willing to let someone help you, rather than pushing them away."

"I don't really do that, do I?"

He chuckled. "You've got more ways to push people aside than anyone I've ever seen."

"But you're the persistent one, right? The one who wants to conquer that in me?"

"Not conquer it. Just prove to you that you can let people in and not get hurt all the time."

"But get hurt some of the time."

"We all get hurt, Deanna. You can't avoid it. It's called life, and sometimes life just knocks you down."

"Like your divorce?"

"Not the divorce. It stung, but it had to be done. But I had other expectations in that marriage, things that I wanted as badly as you wanted to help Emily, and they were taken away from me the way Emily was taken from you.

"And while I'm not equating your tragedy with mine, I just want you to know that I did get hurt, and if it hadn't been for the people I let in, I'd probably still be wallowing in it."

"What?" She asked, turning to face him. "What hurt you that deeply?"

"The betrayal, for starters. And the knowledge that I'd been so oblivious to something everyone around me saw. But most of all…we were in the pre-baby planning stages. At least, I thought we were. But it wasn't working out, she wasn't getting pregnant, and that's when it started to fall apart between us. Or, at least, that's what I tell myself to keep from sounding so utterly stupid. Because we were never, truly together."

"But you wanted a child?"

"Not when she did, but yes. Then when she told me she was…"

"She was pregnant?"

He shook his head. "That's what she said but it was another one of her lies to hold onto me. Or shall I say my wealth."

"But you can't fake a pregnancy. Maybe for a little while, but…"

"She never planned past the first part of it. You know, tell your husband whatever you have to then figure out how to deal with it. Well, when I didn't see symptoms, like morning sickness…"

"I don't get morning sickness."

"Yes, but you don't consume wine either. Or spend time in a hot tub, or tell me you're going to visit your mother when, in fact, you've gone off for some tweaking on your eyelids. She had an elective cosmetic procedure done, and when I found about it, I knew she wasn't pregnant because no reputable plastic surgeon would do that on a pregnant woman."

"I'm so sorry, Beau. It must have been awful."

"Finding out my whole marriage was a lie? Yes, it was awful. But the thing is Brax was there to help me through it. And Joey. I had to let them in, though."

"Which is what I don't do."

"It's not easy."

"But it shouldn't be so hard either. I just don't have much experience."

"Stay here long enough and the whole town of Sugar Creek will embrace you and your baby, Deanna. That's the way the people here are."

"And you're one of those people." She reached over and gave his arm an affectionate squeeze. Then swiped at one stray tear that had held back for a solo journey down her cheek, and sniffled. "Starting with that back massage, I hope."

Beau held up his hands and wiggled his fingers again. "Any time."

"If you have time, how about I grab a quick shower first, then...?" She wiggled her own fingers back at him.

"Sounds good to me." To heck with the time of day, to heck with all the things he had to get done. Giving Deanna a massage suddenly topped his list of things he wanted to do, and that's all that mattered. So he went back to his chair, kicked off his boots again, settled in and listened to the sound of the water hitting the sides of the shower.

Tried hard not to imagine that same water hitting Deanna. She was pregnant, after all. And while he was a man, and *those* thoughts came naturally, he shouldn't be having them. Not now, and especially not about a pregnant woman. But, damn, they wouldn't go away!

"It's getting complicated," she said to the baby as she adjusted the shower spray so she could feel the sting of the water pellets. They invigorated her, would hopefully knock some sense back into her. Whatever was she thinking, melting down in front of him that way? But he'd been so clinical, talking about picking out the perfect *sample* for his horse, talking about wanting to breed a champion. She understood that in the animal world, especially for someone like Beau who loved his horses.

But his clinical example had turned into her personal example when she'd started to wonder if he considered himself the *champion* women would want to father their children. Had that been his reason to donate sperm? If it was, it didn't make sense after how he'd described what he'd gone through after discovering his wife's lie about her pregnancy.

Yes, it was definitely getting complicated. "But I don't think he's like that," she said, laying both hands across her belly. Still, the proof might be in the life she was carrying. Did it really matter why he'd donated? For curiosity's sake, it mattered now more than it had before because…

"Because I know him now. And don't get me wrong," she continued, "you have an amazing daddy. He's someone…" Someone she might have picked for herself. Beau himself. Not his sperm. She liked his devotion to a cantankerous old man. Liked the way he took care of the people in Sugar Creek. Even liked his connection to nature.

Most of all, she liked his sense of duty. Beau tried harder than most people to make his life work in a place he didn't necessarily want to spend his life. Giving up a surgical practice to take on GP duties. Giving up the whole New York experience for quiet little Sugar Creek. All because he was a dedicated man who had a higher sense of obligation that she'd ever seen in anybody else.

"I'm glad he's your daddy, and not…" She bit off her words. No, she didn't have the right to say them out loud. Or even think them. Because that would be disloyal to

Emily, and she'd never, ever do that. Emily had wanted her husband's baby. This was supposed to be Alex's baby. If it had been…

Bad thoughts. Horrible thoughts, and she didn't want them anywhere near her, or the baby. So she turned the shower spray to cold and let the icy water shock her back into reality. "It's going to be fine," she said moments later, while stepping out of the shower. "We're going to figure out how to deal with everything."

But everything was a mess. And the mess was getting bigger. Getting close to Beau had been a mistake. Letting him get close to her was just as big a mistake. She knew that as well. Then working for him on top of everything else?

That's what was on her mind as she pulled on some jersey knit pants and a T-shirt and headed down the stairs, fully aware she was only compounding the mistakes by allowing his fingers to travel the length of her spine. Yet, for now, she didn't care. This wasn't about the baby, it wasn't about anything except…her. God help her, this was what she wanted to do no matter how much she knew she shouldn't.

"If you want my unprofessional opinion, I think you should quit being a doctor and become a masseur." Five minutes and she was already feeling better. For some reason he knew exactly where she hurt. "You've got a fortune in those fingers. I could almost guarantee you instant success, even in a place like Sugar Creek."

He chuckled. "And wouldn't that just give everybody here something to talk about?"

"Until they experienced your fingers. Then they'd know." Yes, they would know. The way they probably knew that she was fixing dinner for Arthur Handler tonight. She'd invited him, he'd accepted, with the stipulation that he'd bring the wine...for himself. And a very pleasing local fruit juice for her. He'd also told her to include Beau in that invitation but so far she hadn't because up until now she'd managed to keep everything just about professional between them. Including this massage: it was necessary for her best performance later on, in the clinic. That's what she was telling herself, at any rate.

"Massages first, then what? A day spa?"

"Nothing wrong with a day spa. I treat myself to one a couple of times a month. It's nice to have somebody pamper you for a few hours." His fingers pressed deeply along the right of her spine and she sucked in her breath then released it slowly. "Lets you... Oh, my...you're on it." Perfectly on it. "That's not going to give me trouble throughout my pregnancy, is it? When I'm bigger?"

"It could. The strain isn't bad, but the more weight you put on your front, the more it's going to pull on your back."

She'd escaped morning sickness, so maybe this was the trade-off. "How long will I be able to have massages?"

"For as long as you want them, provided you find someone who's willing to do them while you're on your side, or even sitting up."

She wanted to ask him if he'd continue with this while she was here, but that was out of line. This was a one-off massage, and anything else turned it into a personal situation. If she wasn't comfortable inviting him to dinner, even with another person there, asking him to work on her back a couple times a week was as far out of the question as it was her comfort zone. But she wanted to. Oh, how she wanted to.

"I'll give my grandson credit where it's due. He was smart to bring you in."

It had been a nice morning, the first part spent with

Beau, the second part reading, and now she was on her way to work, walking across the front yard on her way to the clinic. With Brax tagging along, keeping better pace than she might have expected from a man recovering from a stroke.

"So you weren't against it? Beau led me to believe you don't want anything changing around here."

"In theory, that's right. I don't. It's still my medical practice but nobody seems to remember that. But in practice..." He shrugged. "I can see that some changes might help things. You being one of those changes."

"You do know I'm not here permanently, don't you? I'll be leaving in a month, and Beau's going to have to find someone else to replace me if the two of you can come to an agreement about bringing in outside help."

She'd leave sooner, if she could force herself to leave. It was getting too cozy, too easy, and while she kept telling herself it was temporary, something in her heart was telling her she wanted it to be permanent, that she was in a settling-down kind of mood.

"Maybe even a couple of people because the catchment area of this practice is huge. What happens when he's either up in the mountains seeing Arthur Handler or en route to the hospital? What happens if there's an emergency in Sugar Creek where he's needed, and he's not here?"

"We've always managed."

"You've managed and from everything I hear, you're an excellent doctor. But Beau wasn't educated in your medical system and his first choice in what he wants to practice is not what you've set up here." She opened the front door and held it open as Brax passed through.

"That's not saying that you have to agree with him on everything, or he with you, but you've got to come to some sort of an understanding about who's in charge and who's making the decisions, or Beau will go back to New York and you'll either have to close the practice altogether or bring in a complete stranger. And somehow I don't see that working for you so well."

"So nothing I've done before my grandson took over matters? Is that what you're telling me?"

She went to the blinds and opened them to the view of the mountain, then turned on the light. "Everything you've done here matters. But what Beau's trying to do here matters, too, and you've got to take that into consideration if he decides to stay.

"Honestly, I think he wants to stay, but with the way you keep going at him, that means turning himself into something he never set out to be. You're not making it easy on him by demanding he keep everything the same as it was then fighting him when he makes a change."

"Then he should be the one telling me. *Not you!*"

This wasn't her crisis to solve. But she cared. Deep down, she wanted it to work out for both men because… they were kin to the baby she was carrying, and something about that mattered.

"Maybe he has tried to tell you and you weren't listening." Walking over to alcove where the coffee pot sat empty, she picked it up and went to fill it. "I know your life is disrupted," she said, returning to the waiting area, "and you don't like things the way they are now. But Beau's life is just as disrupted as yours, and none of this is what he wants either."

"Then he should get the hell out and go back where he belongs!" Brax snapped, taking the coffee pot out of her hands and finishing the task of making coffee.

"It's an option, and your attitude is pushing him in that direction. But that's not what you want, is it?"

He stopped for a moment, looked at the loose coffee

he was about to pour into the filter, then sighed. "What I want doesn't matter. Not any more."

"I think Beau giving up his life in New York to be here with you says otherwise. Or *would* say otherwise if the two of you would quit knocking heads. And you're equally guilty on that account, Brax."

"I take it back. He should have never brought you in."

She laughed. "Because I tell the truth, and the truth hurts?"

Plopping the filter into place, he put the pot on the hot plate then stepped away. "Because you're too damned perceptive."

"And women should be seen, not heard, right? And their place is in the kitchen, fixing waffles."

He grudgingly gave in to a smile. "You've got a sharp tongue, young lady."

"And I know how to use it." She arched playful eyebrows back at him

"So you do. Now, what can I do to help you? I've got a free afternoon, and if you really think this clinic needs someone else, I'm the one."

"Is Beau going to go for this?"

"Hell, no. But you'll go to bat for me, won't you?"

Now she was trapped between Beau and Brax. More involvement, more personal conflict to deal with.

"In a limited way, maybe. And that's very limited, Brax, because you still have a way to go before you're ready to step back in fully."

"You mean the cane?" he asked, holding it up.

"Yes, the cane. But also the attitude, the stubbornness. And right now I don't think the two of you could work together. Not without some pretty close..." Deanna smiled sympathetically. "Let's just call it supervision."

"More like refereeing," Beau said from the doorway.

"And, no, he's not working. Do you hear me, Brax?" He raised his voice for emphasis. "You're not working."

She glanced up to see Beau filling the doorframe, and her heart clutched. For a moment she wondered what it would be like to simply stay here and be part of all this. Would she be able to keep the secret and still live her life? That was pure fantasy, pregnancy nesting hormones kicking in.

Still, that's why she'd gotten herself involved in a family struggle that really wasn't any of her business. She wanted to nest. Or settle in. Or sit in front of that massive stone fireplace in the great room up in Brax's house and knit baby booties for the next seven months...even though she didn't know how to knit.

"Is this where the argument begins?" she asked. "Because I may side with your grandfather on this one."

"No arguments right now. Not enough time. Nell's giving birth *right now* and I thought you might want to come and see," Beau said, backing out the door. "Don't have patients coming for an hour yet, so..." He shrugged. "Either of you care to join me?"

"I'd love to watch," Deanna said, turning off the coffee pot and heading out the door behind Beau. With Brax right behind her.

"It's best to watch her quietly from a place where she can't hear or see you," Beau explained, as they entered the next stall over. "A mare gets nervous when too many people hover around, watching. They'd rather give birth where it's secluded and peaceful."

"That's the way I want to do it," Deanna commented, then realized that Beau, Brax and Joey were all staring at her. "It makes sense. Mozart playing in the background, dimmed lights..."

Beau studied her for a moment then smiled. "Nancy always said she wanted to be drugged so hard she wouldn't wake up for a couple of days."

"She wanted designer hospital gowns, too," Brax snorted. "And her beautician on standby. So..." He directed his stare at Deanna. "It's true what they're saying about you?"

"Yes, it's true. I'm pregnant. And just so you'll know right up front, there's no father in the picture."

"Unfortunate," Brax said. "But people are making their various choices these days, aren't they? And single parenting is one of them."

"Single parenting means that when I give birth I'll have the *only* say. Same goes for raising the child as well. That's the beauty part about doing it *without* a significant other. There's no conflict. No one to get in the way."

"Or to hold your hand when you're giving birth or going through a rough patch," Beau said, quietly. "And share the joy."

"Life's always about trade-offs, isn't it?" she said as the miracle of life unfolded quickly in the next stable. It had only been five minutes, and mama was on her side now, with her baby emerging into the world, kicking its way out of its placenta. All so quickly, all so beautifully. And this was going to happen to her.

It was hard to believe that very soon she'd be doing what Nell had just done. Instinctively, her hand slid to her belly. She felt so close to Emily's baby right now. And Beau's baby. That was something she couldn't forget.

"Baby's breathing fine," Joey called over the stall railing. "Everything's looks good. I think we need to give them some bonding time...*alone.*"

Maybe that was true, but Deanna didn't want to leave. Watching something so simple yet so magical caused unexpected emotions to well up inside her. This was a horse...

an animal. And she was already bonding with her baby. Such a natural thing, and it gave Deanna hope that the same kind of instinct would soon take over in her. If not during the pregnancy then at birth, the way it was unfolding with Nell, who was already nuzzling her baby, already being a mother in every way that mattered.

"I'll come back in a little while to make sure everything is going the way it should," Joey said, shooing them out of the stable.

"So, back to the clinic," Brax said, staring Beau straight in the eye.

"What did you say to him?" Beau asked, as Brax set off toward the clinic like a man with a purpose, and they lingered behind.

"Well, for starters, I told him I'm on his side about working. Not a full schedule but something abbreviated. And I told him he's stubborn, and grumpy, and some other things that don't matter."

"Well, you've got the touch. That's all I can say. Something about you has the charm to soothe a savage old doctor."

"I listened to him. It's a simple thing, really. You just put aside your point of view and hear what the other person is saying."

"When you say *you*, you mean…"

"You. Your grandfather is scared of becoming irrelevant. What he sees happening is that you're telling him his clinic already is. Then when you refuse to let him come back to work…"

"But the man has worked all his life. He's got a lot of good years left, and he should be enjoying them, not working through them."

"Unless enjoying them and working through them are

the same things for him. But you've never asked him about that, have you?"

"I don't have to. I inherited his obsession with work, and I'm fighting like hell to get away from some of it because it will destroy everything. I mean, I never even noticed what kind of woman I married. Didn't take enough time to get to know her before the wedding, hardly ever saw her afterwards because I was working damned hard to establish my career.

"My examples in life were Brax and my father, and I turned out to be like Brax, either by heredity or choice. Or a little of both. Either way, I'm fighting against that kind of obsession because I don't want to end up alone and bitter like him."

"Except he's not alone. You're here, and I think that's what he wants."

"Yeah, right. By trying to push me away."

"Or by trying to force you to fit into a system of medical practice he believes won't make him irrelevant." She shrugged. "It's hard being pushed aside. I was raised by good people who took care of my basic needs, but I was an obligation to their family, not a welcomed addition, and I got pushed aside all the time. So I understand where Brax is coming from."

Walking over the grass, she stubbed her toe on a small tree root sticking out of the ground and pitched forward slightly. Before she could right herself, she felt his protective arm slide around her waist then tighten, indicating he wasn't going to let go of her.

And she liked it. Too much. She also wished they could walk much further together like this, rather than the few hundred yards left to them. A little was a lot, though. She was grateful for it. Scared as well.

Mostly, though, she was just enjoying the moment.

CHAPTER SEVEN

"BRAX AND JOEY are staying in for the evening. Brax is sharpening up his scalpel or something, getting ready to go back to work tomorrow after an hour in the clinic learning, or should I say fighting, the computer system, and Joey isn't going too far away from the stables. But I do appreciate the dinner invitation." Beau placed a bottle of sparkling grape juice on the counter then added, "And fifteen minutes is ample notice."

"I thought about inviting you earlier, but then…"

She didn't blame him for being peevish. Letting someone know they were an afterthought would make most people peevish. Except Beau hadn't been an afterthought. In fact, she'd spent the entire day going back and forth on whether or not to invite him, and she'd come close at least a dozen times as they'd brushed shoulders in the clinic.

The only reason he was here now was that Arthur had guilted her into picking up the phone.

"Then I wondered if it was wise to turn a professional relationship into something else."

"Something else? In only a few days you've slipped into my life like nobody ever has before. And not just my professional life. So what the hell do you call that?"

"Making the best of a difficult situation," she responded, much too quickly. "I'm working for you, Beau, and something I never recommend when I consult is fraternization. It makes things…unmanageable when professional turns to personal."

"Good show, Deanna," Arthur quipped from his stool at the kitchen counter. "I'd say you're spot on with that point."

"And this is Sugar Creek, Tennessee. Personal and professional is all one and the same."

"I will say Beau has a point," Arthur commented.

"Which is why the people here in town think you're too stand-offish? Because it's all one and the same?"

"She's got you there, my boy." Arthur twisted to watch them spar.

"That's different. They're patients, and it's always wise to keep a professional distance from your patients."

"Like your grandfather never did?" Arthur asked.

"My grandfather grew up in a different medical era," Beau retorted, but to Arthur, not Deanna. "Back in the day when the good old GP was like part of the family."

"Which doesn't seem bad to me. In fact, I used to look forward to his house calls because I enjoyed a good game of chess and a pleasant hour of stimulating conversation. Which, by the way, I don't get from you. All you do is lecture me about my blood pressure and tell me to cut back on salt or butter. That lecturing is probably why my blood pressure shoots up the moment you walk in the door. You stress me out with your professionalism, son. Which means you're part of my medical problem, not my medical solution."

A huge grin crossed Arthur's face, and to emphasize the rightness of what he'd just said he folded his arms across his chest and simply stared.

It was Deanna who took up the cause, but not by coming to Beau's defense. "Brax put in his first hour today and, with any luck, he'll be able to increase that gradually.

Not sure in what capacity, as I think that's something Brax and Beau have to work out between them. But don't give up on those house calls with chess and lively conversation because they might just happen again."

"Or not," Beau argued.

"Can't you sympathize with your grandfather for a minute? All his years of experience should count for more than struggling with a computer for an hour."

"I sympathize. But can't you also understand that I'm worried?"

"And quite rigid," Arthur interjected. "Which is why Deanna had qualms about inviting you for dinner this evening. You positively emanate stress, which can't be good for her baby."

"Then I should go," Beau said, and immediately headed for the door. But Deanna caught up to him just as he stepped outside.

"That's not what it's about," she said before he reached the steps leading down to the walkway. "Arthur's only trying to protect me, and I appreciate it. But it's not about stress you're causing me. I really did want to invite you, but I do wonder about crossing over the professional line, Beau. I know I've already done that here and…" she shrugged "…it's confusing."

"Why?" He turned to face her. "Why is it confusing?"

"Because I don't get involved that way. When you put yourself into the middle of some kind of personal relationship, expectations start to build. Before you know it, those expectations take root, and they become part of the real you and not just the you who processes them in and out of her life as fast as she can so she won't get hurt. And when I say *you*, I mean me."

"Have you been hurt that much, Deanna?" he asked,

his momentary anger already gone. "Hurt so much or so badly you'd rather be alone?"

"Nobody would rather be alone. That's not how we're made. But…" She glanced in at Arthur, who was making merry with a bottle of wine. He might be a party of one in the world, but nothing about that man smacked of aloneness because he was simply part of the universe and it showed in everything he did.

"But that's how life turns out sometimes, and you can either let it wear you down or make the most of it. The thing is, you've got Brax and all he wants is for you to be there. And you can't see that because you're too busy pushing him aside, like I told you earlier, and convincing yourself it's for your own good."

"I'm not pushing him aside. Just letting him recover. There's a difference."

"Not to Brax there's not. Can you imagine what it feels like to wake up one day with everything ahead of you, and find it all gone the next time you wake up? I know you had a rocky childhood with the way your dad was, but there wasn't a day of it you didn't have that man who's down there, sharpening his scalpels. It doesn't matter who we have. What matters is that we have someone. And you're throwing that away because you're both so much alike.

"What is it about him that you detest or loathe or despise so much that you're not willing to concede even an inch?"

"I don't detest, loathe or despise anyone, Deanna. I love that old man." He swallowed hard. "And I almost lost him. When they called me and told me he'd had a stroke and was in Intensive Care… I had a dad who came and went, did what he wanted whenever he wanted, and I never figured into his life. But Brax, he was…larger than life. Strong. Then he had a stroke and…"

She laid a hand on his arm. "He still is larger than life,

Beau. And strong. You can't protect him from the life he wants, though, and I'm not sure you should. Medicine is what he loves, and all he can see is that you're trying to deprive him of it. Reasons don't matter, and when the emotions are as strong as his, and yours, I'm not even sure the reasons are getting heard."

Her stomach churned over her own words, because Beau had wanted children. She knew that now. And she was having his baby yet depriving him of it. So maybe it was time to tell him and let it be what it was meant to be. Take her own advice and include him. "Um, Beau, while we're on the subject..."

"My blood sugar is getting low," Arthur called through the door. "Wasn't the invitation to include dinner? Or did you two out there forget that I'm in here, practically starving?"

Deanna smiled, partly relieved, partly annoyed.

"Five minutes to get it on the table," she called back, then shrugged apologetically at Beau. But it wasn't a silent apology that he understood, maybe not one he even saw. No matter. There'd be another time. A better time. Or maybe she'd talk herself out of the whole folly and go back to the notion that he'd made an anonymous donation because he'd wanted to be anonymous.

"I did sort of forget he was here," she whispered before they went back into the cabin.

"Of course you did," Arthur quipped. "Parts of me may be going, but my eyes and ears are still very good, my dear. Keep that in mind if you two want to wander off and whisper sweet nothings."

"Not us," Deanna said, swooping past him to grab the salad from the fridge. "We're colleagues and..." She glanced at Beau and smiled. "Just friends."

"Anything you say," Arthur retorted, grabbing a bread-

stick and giving her a smug grin. "As long as you believe
it, that's all that matters, isn't it? But I suppose, as they say,
for a tree to become tall it must grow tough roots among
the rocks. Your roots will grow tough enough to accept
what you need to, my dear."

"Friedrich Nietzsche," she said. "Smart man. But put
away your imagination for a while and take this bowl of
salad over to the table." She pushed it into his hands and
winked at Beau, who was standing in the doorway, simply watching.

"Ah, the course of young love seldom runs smooth,"
Arthur said, as he turned his back on her and headed to
the table. "I dabbled there a time or two in my misspent
youth, maybe a few times since in the subsequent years.
Wouldn't have missed it for the world. In hindsight might
have even done a few things differently. And just for future reference, I don't like being in the middle of a quarrel
among my friends so, please, make love, not war."

He wiggled bushy eyebrows at them as he placed the
salad on the table, then chuckled as he raised his wine glass
to his lips and mumbled his next words into the Cabernet
Sauvignon. "*Just friends*, my wrinkled old ass."

"Up for a walk?" Beau asked.

From the kitchen window, they were watching Arthur's
tail lights descend the mountain road. Amazingly, he was
stone sober. Not even sporting a buzz from the glasses of
wine he'd consumed over the past couple of hours.

In fact, he'd left earlier than they'd anticipated, claiming he was inspired to go and paint night life, whatever
that would turn out to be. Maybe fireflies. Or maybe the
late-night customers trickling into the café in town. Most
likely, though, he was leaving early to give them the rest
of the evening alone.

Which actually sounded nice to her, relaxing with Beau for a while or even taking that walk. But not for whatever Arthur thought might happen. "Maybe. I did eat an awful lot, didn't I? Seriously, two pieces of that strawberry cheesecake Arthur brought with him?" She patted her belly. "I'm blaming it on the mountain air. So, yes, let's go so I can walk off some of the calories."

"In your defense, those pieces of cheesecake were small. And you are—"

She laughed. "Eating for two. I know it and, trust me, I rely on that excuse a lot. But tonight it was pure gluttony. It's nice having friends to share a meal with. Something I rarely ever did back home, unless it was with business associates. And what surprised me about this evening is that you didn't have any house calls or emergencies."

He put the last of the plates in the cabinet and shut the door. "Sometimes that's the way it works out. Or maybe I did some last-minute arranging so I could have dinner with you."

"I really am sorry for the late invitation, but—"

He thrust out his hand to stop her. "I understand. You were applying New York City ways to Sugar Creek. Back in New York I would have done the same thing because you're right, business and personal pursuits don't mix. But it's different here."

"Which is kind of nice, isn't it?"

He smiled. "Most of the time, yes. So, about that walk. There's a place I want to show you. I used to camp there when I was a kid. Actually, I called it running away from home. Brax always knew where I was because he could see my campfire from the house, but I didn't know that. And sometimes, if I didn't build a fire, he'd sneak up to an adjacent ridge just to make sure I was OK."

"You really thought you were getting away with it?"

"In the simple thinking of a child, I *knew* I was getting away with it."

"How long did it take until you went home?"

"Always the next morning. I suppose I thought if I showed up at the breakfast table like I did every morning, Brax would never know I'd run away the night before. And he never mentioned it. Every single time I came back, there he was, sitting at the table, reading his morning paper, drinking his orange juice."

"So, how was the secret revealed? Or was it?"

"I was getting ready to go away for college, going through all the obnoxious things boys do at that age. But things were changing. I was with Brax full time by then, and I knew I'd never see my old man again.

"He wasn't dead, but I just had this sense that it was over and he'd moved entirely into whatever kind of life he wanted. Turned out that was exactly what happened. But at the time, even though I was relieved overall, I was still feeling…abandoned. And dealing with moving away, starting college…rough times.

"Anyway, I went on a little bender, shall we call it. Got myself pretty drunk the night I graduated from high school, ended up in jail. Then, instead of coming to my rescue, the way Brax always had, he left me there. Three days! Thought it might teach me a lesson."

Beau winced at the memory. "Oh, yeah. The food was awful, the cot was awful, there was nothing to do but stare at the walls. Three days of it was all I needed, and when Brax finally came and got me I was angry. Decided to avoid him for a day or two, and went camping at my spot.

"But Brax followed me up this time, said he didn't want to miss the opportunity of running away with me, maybe for the last time. Then he told me how he'd spent nights watching me from the house below, and as often as not from the next ridge over. Said he'd thought about telling me he knew my *secret*, but that sometimes secrets served real purposes."

"How'd you feel about that?"

"A little angry at first that he'd kept it a secret, but overall glad he finally told me because I was mature enough to realize that he had simply been taking care of me the best way he could. When he told me, it became a turning point in our relationship, I think. We went from adult-child to equals, and it was nice."

Hurt, then relieved? Maybe that's the way he'd feel if she revealed the truth about the baby. But deep down she knew that was over-simplifying a matter that was much more complicated than a grandfather looking after his grandson. "Do you believe that secrets can serve real purposes?"

"Only if they're meant to help. Not hurt."

The weight of her secret was getting heavier all the time now, and she wondered about its purpose. Was it changing now that she knew Beau, even had feelings for him? Because right now all she could think about was who would be helped if she told him, and who would be hurt.

Suddenly, Deanna felt emotionally drained, which brought on physical lethargy. "Could we go to your runaway place another time, Beau? It's been a long day, and I'm only now realizing how tired I am. So all I'd like to do is crawl into bed."

"Are you feeling OK?" he asked, instantly concerned.

She shrugged. "Mostly tired." She turned, started to head for the stairs, but as she walked past Beau, he reached out and took her by the hand, and there was nothing in her that could make her pull away from him.

"I do want to be your friend," he said, stepping closer to her. "Not your colleague but your friend. Someone you can trust, or turn to, because I get the sense that you're lost, Deanna, and struggling with something that's bothering you. But I want to help, if you'll let me."

"I appreciate that, Beau. I really do. But it's complicated."

"Any more complicated than asking you to step into the middle of this mess I call my life and fix it?"

She sighed. "That's what I do, though. I fix things."

"You fix everybody else's things. But why won't you let someone help you fix whatever needs fixing in your life? Because I do care, Deanna. Maybe even more than you're comfortable with."

With that, he pulled her into his arms and simply held her. Nothing else. Just wrapped his arms around her and let her lean there, feeling safe and protected. Most of all, feeling cared for. She knew she couldn't have it for ever yet for a few moments she simply wanted to linger and pretend that this was what her for ever could be about. Being held, enjoying the feel of being pressed tight to him. The feel of his muscles, his strength.

It was only when comfort turned to sexual tingling that she pulled back, quite surprised to be having that reaction. Looking up at him, at his face, she saw his smile, and what else? She looked again, wondering if his eyes might be betraying some of that same sexual awareness. Or was she simply misreading a kind act from a kind man? Was she seeing what she hoped to see and not what was there? "I appreciate you wanting to help me but—"

"Try me, Deanna. Just trust me, and try me. You keep telling me that Brax and I need to meet in the middle, but I think you and I need to do that too."

She wanted to. But this was so hard for her. Opening up was so very difficult because no one besides Emily had ever wanted to care, or even listen. She had become proficient in locking it all inside herself.

Beau was genuine, though, and he did want to help her. How far could she go with Beau and not become so overwhelmed with guilt that it affected the baby? Or hurt Beau, if she decided to tell him?

She'd come so close to telling him once, and the longer she put it off, the more difficult it would be. Now it wasn't just about what was best for the baby. It was also about what was best for Beau. It was time to take that first step.

"Look, I owe you some honesty here. What's going on with me isn't about friendship or professionalism, or where or how to draw the line. You're not looking for a relationship and neither am I. So why get ourselves involved in anything other than the ways we're already involved? And I think it would be very easy to get involved, Beau. I'm attracted to you. I won't lie about that. If I were looking for a man in my life, I'd be looking for someone like you. But I'm not in a place yet where I want that kind of involvement because I have...other priorities."

"Wow. When you said you'd be honest, you meant it, didn't you?"

"It's all I have. And I'm sorry. But neither of us is ready for what could happen here. Especially when I tell you the second part of all this."

"Where it gets even more complicated?" he asked. "Because I'd like to respond to the first part before we move on, if I may."

She reached out and gave his hand a squeeze. "You don't have to. I understand that you may be feeling responsible for me because I'm...pregnant. And maybe a little sorry because my life's in an obvious mess. But you don't have to worry about me because I can take care of myself. And I'm sure some of this is about my hormones. Which is why

I want to be honest with you about everything. Because there's more to it, Beau. The baby I'm carrying…"

He stopped her confession when he pulled her hand to his lips and kissed the back of it. Then stepped forward, tilted her face to his and kissed her very gently on the lips. Amazingly, she didn't resist. In fact, she rose up on tiptoe as the kiss lingered on, and twined her arms around his neck. Then thought better of it and pushed back from him.

"I think maybe your hormones might be affecting me too, causing me to have thoughts your hormones might want but I'm not sure you do. Which means it's time for me to go," he said with a wink, as he headed out the door.

"So much for telling him the truth," she said, as her hand slid across her belly. "The thing is, I told him the wrong part of it." The very worst of the wrong part, that she was attracted to him. "So next time kick me," she said to the baby. "When I open my mouth and the wrong things start to come out, kick me as hard as you can. *Please.*"

"When?" Deanna asked. She was too groggy to be coherent, but the shrill voice on the phone was quick to cut through her stupor. She glanced at the clock. Ten after *three*? Seriously? She'd been tossing and turning for hours, thinking about that kiss, the lead-up, its aftermath, and all the things it might or might not imply, trying hard to convince herself it really hadn't meant a thing. So, by her calculation, she'd been asleep only about an hour.

"Did you call Dr. Alexander?"

Somewhere in Janice Parsons's panic what she thought she heard was that Beau wasn't available, and Deanna didn't know what that meant.

"OK, Janice. Listen to me. I don't suppose you know if Lucas has ever done this before." Janice didn't know, and the social workers still hadn't found any relatives to look after him. "OK, I'm on my way. But by any chance, does someone in your family have an inhaler?" No such luck.

"Look, I'm going to run by the clinic, grab some medicine, and I'll be there as fast as I can. In the mean time, have Lucas sit up then try doing something that calms him down, like reading him a story. And call me back... *for anything.*"

By the time she'd clicked off with Janice, she'd pulled on a pair of jeans and a T-shirt, and was on her way to her car, shoes in hand. Once in the car, she dialed Beau and waited until the phone flipped over to voicemail, then left a message. "We have an emergency at Janice Parsons's. Lucas seems to be having an asthma attack. I'm going to grab meds from the clinic and go on out to see him. If you get this, I'll meet you at her place. It's number eleven on Old Mill Road."

She clicked off, curious why Beau wasn't answering. On impulse, she dialed Brax's number. The old man picked up on the second ring.

"Is Beau there?" she asked him.

"He went out on a house call earlier. Horseback. Why?"

"I have a three-year-old having an asthma attack, and I'm on my way to make a house call myself. I'm going to have to stop by the clinic and grab an inhaler or whatever you've got, and I was hoping Beau could go out there with me."

"I'll leave him a message, and in the meantime I'll go on over and get what you'll be needing rounded up," Brax said, then hung up.

Minutes later, after what seemed like the longest drive down the mountain road ever, Deanna pulled up at the clinic and was greeted by Brax and Joey standing at the clinic's front door with supplies—meds, inhalers, portable oxygen. And Brax had his medical bag in his hand as well.

"You don't have to come," she protested, as Joey loaded the supplies into her back seat.

"You don't know the roads, so Joey's going to drive," Brax stated.

"And you?"

"Along for the ride."

"Carrying your medical bag?"

"You've got yours, I've got mine. If Beau shows up, he'll probably bring his. What's the big deal who has what?"

"You're an impossible old man, you know that?" she said, moving over into the passenger's seat as Joey climbed behind the wheel and Brax took his place in the rear. "I can see why Beau gets frustrated. And you know he's likely to kill one, or all three of us, when he finds out you're making a house call at this time of the night."

"Then we won't tell him if he doesn't show up," the old man retorted.

"OK, if you're going to come along, then you've got to listen to me tell you why Beau needs help here. He can't handle it all alone, Brax. He needs someone to run the office. A nurse or medical assistant to help with the medical end of things. And I'm even thinking he could use another doctor. Maybe a specialist like a pediatrician.

"None of this means you won't be able to practice again. But if he keeps up the practice of making house calls, it's not going to be you making these middle-of-the-night runs. So think about the alternatives because something's got to happen, and soon. Even with his mornings off he's working at a crazy, unhealthy pace."

"But I managed all those years and—"

"And you didn't have a life," Joey interrupted. "You worked twenty hours a day and slept four. Which got you where you are now. But Beau's got more sense than that."

"Everybody's ganging up on me," Brax snorted. Then

he went silent for the rest of the trip to Old Mill Road, and Deanna hoped he was considering all sides of Beau's dilemma. Because if he wasn't, and he truly couldn't see the value in bringing in others to work with Beau, this wasn't going to be a solvable situation. Which meant that Beau *would* return to New York and Brax would have to sell his practice to someone else.

It wouldn't make anybody happy. Not Brax, not Beau. And, for some strange reason, not even her. To see it end would be sad.

CHAPTER EIGHT

JANICE PARSONS'S HOUSE, where every single light was on, was shining like a beacon on a very dark, secluded road. "He's breathing better," Janice said, running up to the car before Deanna had a chance to get out. "But I can't do this. I have my own kids to take care of, and this scared them to death."

"Where is he?" Deanna asked, trying to ignore the woman's panic.

"Upstairs, second door on the right. My husband's with him."

Her husband, a huge lumberjack-looking man, was sitting in a rocking chair with Lucas, who was audibly wheezing but not in the throes of a very bad attack. When Deanna approached them, the man said nothing but simply stood and handed over the boy then exited the room.

"Lucas," Deanna said, setting him down on the bed. "Are you feeling better?"

Huge tears welled in his eyes and he sniffled in a ragged breath but didn't say a word.

"He doesn't talk," Janice said from the doorway. "Doesn't eat. Doesn't interact with my children. And now this...I don't know what to do for him." Her panic had given way to discouragement. "I can't keep him any longer, Miss Lambert. He's taking too much time away from my children, and…"

Deanna nodded then waved Janice off, not to be rude but to be silent while she listened to Lucas's chest. There was definitely some pronounced wheezing going on bilaterally, but nothing as bad as she'd expected, and she wondered if Janice had overreacted or exaggerated simply because she was at her wits' end.

"Lucas," she said, pulling her stethoscope out of her ears, "do you know what this is?" She pulled an inhaler out of her pocket and showed it to the boy, but he neither looked at it nor did he respond. So she forged on. "It's going to help you breathe better. When I put the white part in your mouth, I'd like you to take a deep breath. Can you do that for me?"

Again there was no response. But she needed him to acknowledge, in some way, that he knew what she was about to do. "Lucas, look at me. This is very important. I want to give you something to help you breathe, but I need to know if you understand what to do. Can you take that deep breath for me when I put the white part in your mouth? You don't have to swallow it or anything. Just wrap your lips around it. Can you do that for me?"

Again there was no real response except a quick glance at her. One fast look then his eyes were cast downward again. But that's all she needed. Her opening. He was listening and he did understand. The rest of it was about one very sad little boy who missed his mommy and daddy, and while her memories were dim, she did recall feeling the way Lucas had to be feeling. "OK, just open your mouth a little for me, and…" When he did, she slipped the inhaler mouthpiece just past his lips. "Take a deep breath for me, Lucas. A very deep breath."

The boy obeyed, and on cue Deanna pumped the bronchodilator into him. "Now, let me count to twenty for you, and when I get to twenty, that's when your breathing will start to get better. OK?" Of course, it didn't work that quickly, or that easily, but if he believed it did, she was home free.

He nodded, so she started to count. "One...two...three..."

"And you said you were afraid you might not have the right natural instincts to be a mother," Beau said from the doorway.

"Thirteen...fourteen...fifteen..."

"I think you've got it all," he continued.

"Nineteen...twenty. Now, is your breathing better?" she asked.

Lucas didn't look up but he did nod in the affirmative.

"Good, now I want you to scoot back and lean against the pillows, and just rest there for a few minutes. Can you do that for me, Lucas? Rest against the pillows, sitting up. It's important that you stay sitting up."

"His vital signs?" Beau asked, stepping into the room.

"Blood pressure a little up, respirations and pulse a little up. Nothing critical. And your grandfather was the one who technically prescribed the bronchodilator, if that's what you're worried about."

"My grandfather is engaged in a game of checkers with one of the kids downstairs, trying to keep Janice from having an asthma attack herself she's so stressed. And, no, I wasn't worried about you using an asthma drug. I'm glad you took the call. I was out seeing Mrs. Gardner. She's close to seventy, her husband died recently, and she occasionally has rough nights being alone...panic attacks. Apparently she's in a dead zone for cell reception."

"But she's better?"

Beau nodded. "For tonight. And Lucas?"

She glanced at Lucas, who was staring out the window

next to the bed. "It wasn't a serious attack but Janice wasn't going to take no for an answer."

Beau motioned Deanna into the hall. Lowering his voice, he said, "And she's not going to let Lucas stay here any longer."

"I guessed that's where this was leading so somebody will have to call Social Services."

"No, that's not what I'm saying. When we leave here in a little while, Lucas is going with us. Janice won't keep him, not even for the rest of the night."

"What will we do with him?"

Beau shrugged. "I'm hoping you'll take him until morning."

"Me?" She didn't know how to take care of a child outside her capacity as a nurse. She had no idea what a three-year-old was about, unless someone wanted a dissertation on the anatomical structure of a three-year-old. But surrogate mother duties? They were coming soon enough to her and she didn't want to bring that deadline forward until she'd learned more, read more, watched more videos. "I think he'd be better off with you."

"He's responding to you. Look at him, he's watching you, not me."

It was true. He was. "But, Beau, I..." She shook her head. "I can't..."

"Sure you can. Just pretend it's three years from now and this is your child who needs to be cared for."

Caring for Emily's baby three years in the future... that's the thought that calmed her down, made her realize that motherhood was going to be thrust upon her one way or another, and very soon. So why not get some pre-mothering in now? "The cabin does have one bedroom for kids. I suppose I could manage it for the rest of the night."

"Possibly part of tomorrow."

She looked back in at Lucas, who was still staring at her. Big blue eyes so lost it broke her heart, curly blond hair so cute she wanted to tousle it. As she watched him for few moments, something stirred in her, something profound and unexpected because, suddenly, all she wanted to do was take him back to the cabin and tuck him into bed. No more hesitation, no more worry.

The mothering instinct welling in her was turning fierce, and doing so very quickly. Sure, it was the batting back and forth of her hormones but that didn't change what she wanted, which was having that little boy in her arms. "How can that happen so fast?" She asked, not meaning to say it out loud.

"What?" Beau asked.

"The way my switch turns on and off. One minute I can't take him home, the next minute I want to so badly I'm about ready to knock you over to get to him."

He chuckled. "One of the beautiful things about pregnancy is it's unpredictable."

"Guess that's good because I do want to take him. But they've got to find his family, Beau, because he needs to be settled in." A feeling she remembered having about something she'd never had when she'd been a child. Still didn't, even now.

"Then I'll make sure the proper authorities know where he is."

"How did you know we were here?" she asked, before she went back to gather up Lucas and his few belongs that had been salvaged from the car wreck.

"Got myself out of the dead zone."

"Well, you need a better way to communicate if you're going to wander around the mountains at night, or any other time. I was worried. Oh, and by the way, I had a little talk with your grandfather about some practical matters regarding the medical practice."

"And?"

"He's not talking to me right now, but he didn't thump me with his cane either, so I guess that's a good sign."

Beau reached across, brushed her cheek with his thumb and smiled. But he didn't respond so to fill in the awkward silence between them, she continued, "Anyway, let me go grab Lucas and get him out to the car. And round up Joey and your grandpa, too."

"Joey's already taken the horse back to the stables... short cut through the woods. So you're stuck with me."

Stuck with Beau...there were times that didn't sound so bad. But that didn't block out the fact that she'd tossed and turned for three hours because the only thing looping through her mind had been one terrifying question: what would it be like to stay here and be close to Beau? Or even, in some distant part of the wildest of imaginations, be *with* Beau.

Because, yes, she was falling for him. Which was giving way to senseless notions and absurd schemes as there was still one huge obstacle to overcome—telling him that the baby she was having was his. However was that going to work out?

Right now, she just didn't know.

"OK, Brax is settled back at the house and Lucas is tucked in upstairs. So what about you? Are you ready to be tucked in?"

"Again. Tucked in again," she said. Too tired to trudge into the bedroom, she slumped into the overstuffed sofa in front of the fireplace. "I was tucked in before."

"No doubt sleeping like a baby."

"No doubt," she said, yawning. "But I'm going to stay

up for a while, in case Lucas wakes up. He's in a strange bed, in a strange house, staying with people he doesn't know, and he doesn't understand it because his world has changed into a big, scary place. So I want to stay close by." She smiled. "Be a little over-protective."

"That's the natural instinct you were afraid you didn't have," he said, smiling.

She stifled a yawn and laughed. "I hope you're right. Especially for Lucas right now. I mean, I know what's it like to wake up in the middle of the night and be so scared you don't know what to do, and you don't have anybody to turn to. Which is why I'll stay up, in case Lucas wakes up."

"Which is why *I'll* stay up," Beau corrected. "You're exhausted, and you need the rest. And before you think you can win this argument, you're sleeping for two."

"Not fair," she said.

He smiled as he extended a hand to help her up off the sofa. "All's very fair. You came to Sugar Creek for one reason, and I'm taking up all your time with things I'm supposed to be doing. The least I can do is let you sleep the rest of the night, uninterrupted. Oh, and sleep late in the morning as well. Doctor's orders."

The feel of his hand was so...so comforting. Smooth. Strong. His kiss, his touch... This was getting serious now. And she was too confused to figure out how to handle it. So, for the moment, she wouldn't. "Well, if the doctor insists," she forced herself to say as she moved past him, refusing to do so much as even look up at him.

"The doctor insists. And, Deanna..."

"Yes?" Approaching the stairs, she stopped and finally looked into his eyes. But he didn't say anything. He simply smiled, then nodded.

And what she'd known only moments earlier was now confirmed. She'd gone and done the wrong thing. The worst thing. The most stupid thing. Yet the most wonderful… Except now she had to figure out a way to undo it. "I'll see you in a few hours," she said, then turned, practically flew up the stairs and shut the bedroom door behind her. Locked it. Yet still felt more vulnerable than she'd ever felt in her entire life.

Yes, she had to figure out a way to undo the mess. And undo it fast.

Beau watched Lucas, who sat at the breakfast table much too quietly for a toddler. His heart ached for the little boy but physically there was nothing wrong with him and emotionally nothing he could do for him. He felt powerless and discouraged. He hated seeing anyone suffer this way, but watching a child going through this was the worst.

He'd known abandonment himself—the death of his mother, a father who had wandered in and out, a wife who'd had her own agenda. In an adult way he understood these things, understood the pain they'd caused him. But Lucas had no basis for understanding, no basis for knowing what the awful pain meant.

"At that age you loved to ride with me," Brax commented. He'd come up to the cabin for breakfast earlier, at Beau's invitation. "In fact, every time I walked out the door, you were hanging on my leg, begging me to take you on a horsey ride."

Beau remembered that. "And that little *horsey* song you'd sing to me." *If I had a horsey, you know what I'd do?* It had been a purely a made-up little song to soothe a distressed child, but it had been Brax's cure for all those times Beau's dad had dropped him off for an hour or two and hadn't come back to get him for a week or two.

"The horses cured so many things for me. Made things seem better. And you always saw that, didn't you?" They'd given him the confidence his dad had taken from him. Confidence and purpose. But all that had really come from Brax.

"Well, I saw how you always lit up when you saw them so I used some common sense."

"More than common sense, Brax. Way more than common sense." Impulsively, he crossed the room to his grandfather and gave the man a hug, then a kiss on the cheek. No words. Just the loving gesture. "I don't know if Lucas has ever seen a horse. According to his parents' identification, they were from Chicago, and the last time I was there, I don't recall seeing any horses within city limits, so maybe this will be a good experience for him."

The way it had been a good experience for Beau. "But maybe you could take him down to the stables later, like you used to do for me?"

"Me? Are you sure about that?"

Beau chuckled. "You have a way with children, old man, so don't push it, OK?"

"Me, push anything? Not a chance, but you'd better watch it because that nurse you hired is the pushy one. Damned pushy."

Beau simply shook his head then grabbed two glasses of orange juice and carried them over to the table.

"So, does anybody know what the boy's parents were doing here?" Brax asked.

"According to the police report, they'd rented a cabin for a couple of weeks, but somewhere closer to the North Carolina border."

"Damn shame what happened. And you said the authorities haven't turned up any relatives yet?"

Beau shook his head on his way back to the stove to grab the platter of fresh pancakes he'd just cooked and carry them over to the table. "Not yet. But they're still looking." Then, under his breath, he said, "Hope they find someone soon. I don't like the idea of him having to go into foster-care, but that's what might happen."

"No way in hell!" Brax snapped, also under his breath. "That boy needs family who care about him. And if they think they're going to put him in the guardian home or with a foster-family...no way in hell!" he snapped again. "I've got a big house and he's welcome there."

He picked up the maple syrup container, took it to the table, sat down then slathered more maple syrup on his stack of pancakes than one human being had a right to eat at any one sitting.

"I mean it, Beau. I'm not too old to take care of him, if that's what it comes down to." Then he scooted a plate with one pancake on it towards Lucas and placed the syrup bottle next to it. "Losing a parent is a tragedy, but being all alone..." He shook his head. "I'm not going to allow the boy to face that with strangers."

"Seriously, you'd let him stay with you?" he asked, thinking back to all those times he'd been the little boy abandoned on the side of the road with his blanket and told to walk down the driveway until he got to his grand-father's house.

It had been a short walk, maybe just a quarter of a mile, but to a scared five-year-old dragging his blanket down that dusty drive it had turned into the longest walk in the world. And he'd been dumped out of his father's car to take that walk so many times. But Brax had always been there to take him in.

"I'd let him stay with us, Beau. *Us*, because we both understand..."

Both men watched quietly for a moment as Lucas looked at the pancake then tentatively picked up the syrup bot-tle and mimicked Brax by pouring on way too much. But that's all he did. Once the syrup was dripping over the edges of the plate, Lucas put the syrup bottle back on the table and simply stared at the drippy, sticky mess. Didn't attempt to eat it, didn't even attempt to play in it, which caused Beau even more worry. At that age what child could, or would, resist playing in such a puddle of goop?

"If they were looking for *my* relatives," Deanna said on her way down the stairs, "they wouldn't turn up anybody, because I don't have anybody. Maybe some very distant cousins but nobody close enough to be considered real family. I wondering if that could be the case here. Hope it isn't, though."

"Thought you were going to sleep late," Beau said, diverting his attention to Deanna for a moment and noticing the way the morning sun streamed in through the window and framed her every step down the stairs. She was the picture of perfect grace and beauty, and he couldn't help but stare.

Feelings for the little boy, feelings for the pregnant nurse…domesticity was practically strangling him this morning. The implication of it made the first few bites of pancakes turn into lumps of cement in his gut. What the hell was he doing, anyway?

"For me, this is late. Besides, I smelled some mighty fine aromas floating up the stairs, and it's not every day I find someone in my kitchen cooking for me." She acknowledged Brax with a smile then looked at Lucas, who was simply staring at his pancake.

"Someday, Lucas," she said, as she approached the massive, hand-carved pine log table, "you're going to want to impress a lady, and cooking for her is a nice way to do that. But not with so much syrup."

She reached over to take away his plate but he grabbed it out of her hands and moved it right back to the spot in front of him. He didn't say a word but the angry look he gave her spoke volumes.

"Our guest seems to have a temper," Beau commented, setting another plate with a stack of pancakes on the table and gesturing for Deanna to sit.

"Well, if he insists on keeping that pancake, he's going to have to eat it. So, can you cut it up yourself, Lucas, or do you want me to do that for you?" Before the boy had a chance to answer, if he'd even been inclined to answer, Deanna took his fork and cut several bite-sized pieces then paused to see if he had any reaction. None, outside of watching, so she handed him the fork to see what he'd do.

The answer to that came in about two seconds when he hurled the fork across the room. Two seconds later the plate followed, spilling pancake and syrup and shattering the plate into thousands of tiny glass shards. Which left Beau and Deanna staring at each other, clearly wondering what to do, while Brax ignored the whole thing and simply continued to eat.

And Lucas…again there was no response, except for the huge tears rolling down his face.

Instinctively, Deanna scooped him up into her arms, cradled him and rocked him as his silent tears turned into sobs that racked his tiny body.

Nobody in the kitchen said a word. Beau simply stood there, feeling more helpless than he could ever remember feeling, and even Brax quit eating when the lump in his own throat grew so large he couldn't swallow.

"Shh," Deanna whispered to Lucas as she stroked his hair. "It's going to be all right, sweetheart. Everything's going to be all right."

No, it wasn't. Beau knew that for Lucas Dempsey nothing was going to be right for a long, long time, and there wasn't a thing he could do about it. But bless Deanna for stepping in the way she was. He was holding onto her for dear life. And somehow he didn't think Lucas was going to have to come and stay with him and Brax. He was already where he was going to stay for the next little while.

"You're safe here, Lucas," she continued. "Beau and Brax and I are going to take good care of you."

"Or just Deanna," Beau said.

"Why just me?"

"Because he's responding to you and you're responding to him. Because you're turning into a nurturer, and he needs nurturing. Because doing the family thing isn't for me. Take your pick."

Because it all scared him to death—getting attached, having it ripped away. He wanted what was best for Lucas and he'd absolutely take him in, if that's what it came down to, but the noose of domesticity was getting even tighter and Deanna's affection for the boy was the solution. So why not take advantage of it? It was good for her, good for the boy…perfect situation that would let him breathe freely again.

Deanna gave him a curious look but didn't say anything. She simply stared at him like she was staring at a stranger.

"What?" he finally asked.

"Nothing. Just…" She shrugged. "Nothing."

Was it his imagination or did Deanna look…sad? Maybe even a little angry, although she was trying hard to hide it. "It's best for Lucas," he finally said.

She nodded, didn't speak.

"And you know Brax and I will do whatever we can to help you."

Again a nod but no words.

"Better not open your mouth again, son," Brax warned. "You've already got both feet in it, don't think there's room for anything else, like that crow I think you're about to have to eat."

"I was just saying—"

"That's the problem," Brax continued, "So quit *just saying* while you're ahead. Actually, you're not ahead, so quit saying it before you fall any further behind."

"No, it's fine," Deanna interjected. "If Beau doesn't want to do the family thing…"

"Big crow to eat," Brax mumbled. "Big, *big* crow."

"How about I let you two men stay here and talk it out, fight it out or do whatever you do while Lucas and I go down to the town and start over with breakfast?" She deliberately turned away from them to devote her full attention to the boy. "What would you like for breakfast, young man?" she asked him. "What's your favorite thing to eat in the morning?"

"Cereal," he said, his voice muffled into her chest.

"Then I think we need to go to the café and buy you some cereal. After that, we'll go to the store and you can pick out a box of your favorite. Will you do that with me, Lucas?"

"Uh-uh," he said.

"And maybe we can find a game you'd like to play. And some books we can read. Does that sound like fun?"

"Uh-uh."

She glanced at Beau. "I'd invite you to come along but what we're going to do is pretty much one of those *family things*."

It was said with so much ice it immediately chilled him to the bone. It was obvious he'd said the wrong thing, but in his defense it was his reaction to feelings he didn't want to have, feelings that were pushing their way in despite his best effort to push them away.

"You got that crow handy," he said to Brax as Deanna

and Lucas headed out to the car, "because I think I'm going to be gnawing on it for a while."

"Or just admit what you're feeling?" Brax suggested.

"You mean confused?"

"What's confusing? You're falling in love with her, aren't you?"

Beau shrugged. "I don't know what I'm doing."

"And the fact that she's pregnant doesn't matter?"

"It does, but not the way you think." The facts of her pregnancy were for her to divulge if she wanted to. As far as he was aware, Brax didn't know. "More than anything, I admire her for what she's doing."

"Look, son, I know that Nancy really messed you up with her motives and pretending to be pregnant. But that's the past. You need to put it behind you or, mark my words, you'll regret letting someone like Deanna get by you. Don't you think you owe it to yourself to get just a little involved with her? Or even see if there's a reason to think about getting involved?"

"I'm not shopping for women," Beau snapped.

"Didn't say you were. But let's just say that you never were very good keeping secrets from me. It was always in your eyes, son. And what I'm seeing there when you look at her…" He shrugged. "Never saw it there for Nancy. That's all I'm saying."

Beau shut his eyes. "I'm not ready. I just can't do it again," he said, fighting back the images of Deanna that kept popping into his head. "Deanna may be the best thing I'll never know, but…" Opening his eyes, he shrugged. "She deserves more than someone who doesn't remember how to trust. And I just can't remember what it was like before Nancy happened to me. Besides that, Deanna's not interested. She told me so."

"That's what you're saying, too, but look how interested

you *really* are. Could be the same with her. Either way, you'll remember what you need when you need it. Until then, one step at a time, and that first step is out the door. Go fix what you broke with Deanna, even if you aren't going to take a step closer than that, because you're not the kind of man who'd let it slide by.

"She's quality through and through, son, and pretty damned tolerant of putting up with everything we've thrown at her since she got here. So go set it straight with her, and let me finish my breakfast in peace. Will you?"

"One step," Beau said.

"But you'd better make it a pretty damned fast one, because she's already halfway off the mountain. Deanna's the real deal. Nancy was only a cheap imitation."

Deanna was more than just the real deal, he was coming to realize. She was the *only* deal. But as clear as that was to him, he still didn't know what to do about it. One way or another, though, everything in his life was about to turn over in ways he couldn't anticipate. Given his present confused state of mind, he wasn't sure he wanted to.

Although in his true heart, he knew. He absolutely knew.

CHAPTER NINE

IT HAD TO be the hormones, because now she was embarrassed about the way she'd reacted to Beau's pronouncement that he didn't want to do the family thing. It was his choice, probably for very good reasons. And it was none of her business. Still, hearing those words from the father of the baby inside her had evoked a strong, fast emotion she hadn't expected. He'd hurt her feelings. Granted, the circumstances weren't normal. Not anywhere close to normal. But she'd reacted the way she might have if they were in a relationship, which was just plain senseless.

"I could ask around and see if someone else could keep him until the social workers figure out what to do," Kelli Dawson suggested. She'd slid into the booth across from Deanna the instant Deanna and Lucas had ordered breakfast cereal, and right now Lucas was pressed so tightly into Deanna's side it was hard for her to move.

"No, we're fine. I don't think shuffling him off to yet another situation is a good idea. And I've got Beau, Brax and even Joey to help me. And Lucas...well, we get along. We understand each other, I think. I want to keep him if I can until his permanent situation is arranged."

Funny how she was almost picturing Lucas as part of her little family. Her, Emily's baby and Lucas. And... No! She wasn't inserting Beau into that scenario. That was too much of a family thing to do. "We're good," she said, holding a little tighter to the boy.

"Strange how life works out, isn't it? A few days ago you didn't know any of them, and now look at you, all involved."

Yes, just look at her. *All* involved. "Just going with the flow," she said, as the server brought Lucas's cereal to the table.

"Sure I can't get you something?" the server asked her.

A little unexpected queasiness had set in, just when she'd thought she'd escaped the whole morning sickness process. Nothing substantial. Not even in proportions she'd attribute to what she'd always believed morning sickness would be. But what she was feeling right now didn't seem like it would connect so well to food, so she opted for a cup of hot tea with a single slice of toast, with the hope she could force herself to eat it.

"Just the tea and toast," she said, picking up the small pitcher of milk on the table and pouring it over Lucas's cereal.

"I got that way with my first two," the server said. "Didn't want to eat a thing. Lost a few pounds in my first three months, then went on to make up for that after the morning sickness was over. Toast works. And when you leave here, I'm going to send some saltine crackers with you because they're good for morning sickness, too."

"You're pregnant?" Kelli asked, sounding surprised.

Well, the cat was certainly out of the bag now. "Right at two months." She tried forcing a smile, wondering how fast the news would spread.

"Is it good for you, or bad?" she asked, as the waitress, whose name was Jane, stepped in a little closer to hear the details.

"Good. Very good. I made the decision to do it…" She

shrugged then took a deep breath. "Do it the way I'm doing it."

"All alone?" Kelli asked, sounding like she couldn't bring herself to believe that someone would make the choice to be a single parent.

"All alone. Single mom." She glanced down at Lucas, who was simply staring at his cereal. He was holding onto the spoon with a grip so tight his little knuckles were turning white, but there was nothing in his eyes to suggest he even knew the bowl of cereal was sitting in front of him. "And very happy about it."

"Well, good for you," Jane said, giving Deanna a squeeze on the shoulder. "You're going to be a terrific mother. And you can count on the people in Sugar Creek to help you out when the times comes."

Apparently Jane didn't know she was a temp here. The offer of help and support sounded wonderful, though. And very tempting. "I think the help I need most right now is trying to find a way to get Lucas to eat. Beau made pancakes for breakfast this morning but Lucas wouldn't touch them. So I brought him here for cereal because he said it's what he wanted, and now…"

Kelli and Jane turned their attention to the boy, who'd twisted around to stare out the window. "My son is about his age," Kelli said. "Maybe a little older. Do you think he'd like to come over and play this afternoon?

"My husband's built a play fort, which Max dearly loves, and we'd planned on lunch and games in the fort later on. We turn it into a scavenger hunt, hide little things around the yard for Max to find, then when he does he has to tell us what they're used for. It's a teaching game, actually. My husband is an elementary school teacher, so we're all about education."

"I don't know if Lucas is up to it," Deanna said. "But

that might work out as I need to go on duty at one. At least it would give him a chance to be around someone closer to his own age, which will probably be good for him because he's surrounded by adults right now. That can't be much fun, can it, Lucas?" she asked. "Not having somebody your own age to play with."

Lucas responded with a shrug then leaned his head against the back of the bench seat and closed his eyes. She knew he was past most of the crying now. This was despondency. He was sinking into a well of depression and for someone so young, that was dangerous.

She understood it better than anybody but Lucas could know. And what she also understood was that he did need some normalcy in his life, because at his age that would distract him for a little while. And even the smallest distractions counted. "What time do you want me to drop him off?" she asked.

"On your way to work is fine. I've got one appointment this morning then I'll be home for the rest of the day, and since this is summer holiday, David's there all day."

"Chocolate milk," Jane piped up. "I think Lucas needs a big glass of chocolate milk. Don't you, Lucas?"

Surprisingly, Lucas turned his head, looked at her for a moment then very quietly, said, "Yes, please."

"Amazing," Deanna said.

"Not amazing. Just years of experience, three children and five grandchildren." She bent down closer to Deanna and whispered, "And it's not really chocolate milk. One of my grandchildren is a picky eater so I keep a childhood supplement on hand. It's full of essential vitamins and it fools her every time. So let me run home and get a can..."

"You don't have to do that," Deanna said.

"It's just down the street. Be right back." She pulled off her apron and tossed it across the food counter to a perky, fiftyish redhead with a name tag that read "Cathy", then bounded out the door.

"She can just leave like that?" Deanna asked Kelli.

But her answer came from Beau, who'd walked in at the same time Jane had exited. "One of the advantages of living in a town like Sugar Creek is that you don't have the same rules. Nice place to raise a child, actually."

He'd followed her to town, and seeing him standing at the end of the booth, knowing that he'd come there for her, caused her pulse to speed up. "Shouldn't you be out at the stables?" she said, as Cathy brought over the cup of hot tea and the toast she'd ordered. Problem was, it seemed even more unappetizing to her now than it had been when she'd ordered it just a couple of minutes ago.

"I was, but I think I gave you a wrong impression and I wanted to clear it up." He glanced at Kelli and smiled. "By the way, I may have someone who's interested in buying the cabin overlooking my grandfather's place. The one where Deanna's staying. It comes with all the acreage all the way down the side of the mountain, doesn't it?"

"About seventy-five acres, total. Adjoining your property." She fished a business card from her purse and handed it to him. "Please, have him or her call me. I've got a motivated seller." She glanced at Deanna. "Not you, is it?"

"Afraid not. In fact, as we speak, I've got an agent back in New York who's looking for a new apartment for me. Sorry."

"I was really hoping you'd stay. Doc Beau is right," Kelli said as she scooted off the bench. "This is a nice place to raise a kid. Look, I'll see you around one. And, Lucas, think of some things you'd like to do this afternoon. Maybe go wade in the creek? Or take a hike in the woods?"

"Lucas has an outing planned?" Beau asked, as Kelli

took her leave and Jane re-entered the diner with the fortified chocolate children's beverage she was calling milk.

"While I'm working."

"You don't have to work, Deanna. Brax is ready to manage the office."

"And Brax isn't a nurse. You need medical help, which he's not ready to do yet, except in very minor cases."

"And you need to get back to what you came here to do in the first place."

Outside the actual work she'd brought along, everything important she'd come to do had already been done. She knew as much as she needed to know about the baby's father, including that he didn't want children.

Should she tell him the baby was his or not? Somehow she'd been wandering around in a fuzzy fantasy where she would tell him, he'd be thrilled, and their lives would forever intertwine. That wasn't going to happen, though. Her life was going to be wrapped up in something he didn't want, and there was nothing she could do about it. Not on her side of it, not on his.

So while she might have convinced herself into believing she had some feelings for Beau, she'd have to convince herself right back out of it.

"My client came to a conclusion on how to proceed with the problem, so nothing else is required except to implement the plan." And that was the hard part. For, as much as she knew what she had to do, nothing in her was pushing in that direction. Not yet, anyway. "So except for a few loose ends to tie up, I'm...free." She looked at Lucas.

"But I'm going to hang around for a while until we get *this* situation taken care of because I'm discovering I like doing the family thing."

"We need to talk about that. *I* need to talk about that because—"

"Chocolate milk," Jane interrupted, setting the cup down in front of Lucas, who came to life long enough to pick it up and take a few sips.

"Good?" Deanna asked.

He answered with a nod. Then went back to staring out the window. But this time he continued drinking.

"It's a miracle," Jane pronounced. "And if you don't get some of that toast in you, I'm going to go home and get *you* a can of my special chocolate milk."

Chocolate didn't sound good at all. In fact, the mere thought of it forced Deanna to break a corner off the piece of toast and stuff it in her mouth, hoping it would dissolve before she actually had to chew it.

"Nausea?" Beau asked.

"A little. Probably a hormonal swing."

"Or a vitamin B deficiency, or stress. Carrying twins or triplets might cause more nausea than normal."

"Twins?" Deanna asked.

"Or triplets?" Jane interjected. "Don't recall knowing anybody who's had triplets."

Deanna shook her head. "Not twins." Although the doctor who'd done the implant procedure had mentioned the possibility. But she'd never thought in terms of having twins. Emily had wanted a child, and in Deanna's mind that's what the outcome had been. Still…

"How long since you've had an exam?" Beau asked her.

"Not so long that you're going to do one on me," Deanna said, forcing herself to take a second bite of the toast while forcing herself to *not* think about twins.

"You haven't had an ultrasound yet, have you?"

"It's scheduled for when I go back to New York."

"In a month."

"A month. But I think you should find out sooner, considering…" He glanced at Jane, who had wedged herself in even closer, trying her discreet utmost to hear every word. "Considering," he repeated, and didn't qualify it further.

"He's a good doctor," Jane said. "Almost as good as his grandpa is. I know you're a nurse, but if I were you I'd do what he says."

"Except there's no convenient way to have that done around here, is there?" she said, feeling like she was being put under a microscope, with all the attention she was getting.

"My helicopter will get us to a real medical center in no time at all. And all I have to do is make a phone call to get you a referral to an obstetrician."

"If that's what I want to do. But it isn't, Beau. I'm capable of handling my situation very well on my own. And the nausea is a passing thing." She popped a large piece of toast into her mouth like that was going to prove something then fought to swallow it.

But the gag reflex got her and by the time she'd slid from the booth she knew she'd made a big mistake. "Watch Lucas," was all she managed to get out before she dashed to the restroom.

"Brave young lady," Jane said as she finally went to wait on another customer. "Too bad she's alone, going through this. But we all make our choices, don't we?"

"Yes, we do," Beau said, his focus clearly on something that wasn't visible. "We all make our choices. Then, good or bad, we have to live with them."

As far as patient care went, the afternoon was light, although there were a few scattered people to see this evening. No one too far away, though, and Beau was definitely beginning to see some advantages to encouraging a few more of his patients to come to the clinic rather than him going to them.

House calls were taking up a lot of his time, especially on an evening like this where he'd rather spend his time relaxing with Deanna here on the porch. Making things right between them again. But he had an hour then he was off to tend a case of bronchitis, a suspected bout of gout, and a chronic bellyache that was always caused by greasy food. Would have been a perfect night to settle in, though.

"So tomorrow morning we'll fly in early, you'll have your exam, and we'll be back before noon." Beau handed Deanna a glass of lemonade, and sat down on the porch swing next to her. "Brax will look after Lucas and—"

"And you'll be the pilot?" she asked.

"Unless you want to be."

"Why are you doing this?" Deanna asked him. "Not just getting me to an obstetrician for an ultrasound but everything? It's like you're settling into that family thing you don't want to be part of."

"I really misspoke. That was some of the ugly sentiment lingering from my marriage, which always seems to pop up at the worst times. But it was hell, Deanna. And I was so damned blind to it all..." He gave a deep sigh. "What does that say about me? What does it say about my ability to have the kind of perception and strength a family would need from me?"

"It's not about your perception or strength, Beau. It's about your trusting nature, which is a good thing. It's about the way she hurt you because you trusted her."

"Trusted her... On the days she was ovulating, she'd call me, beg me to come home. If I couldn't she'd come to the hospital and just barge in. I felt guilty because I knew I was leaving her alone too much, and I thought she was reacting to that loneliness as much as anything else. But what she did... I was just, plain stupid."

"We all see what we want to in various situations. You

were busy and ambitious, and you believed that was what made her so needy. I can understand that."

"So it's not the family thing I don't want. Even though I wasn't sure I was ready for a family at the time she was trying to get pregnant, I was ecstatic when I thought she *was* pregnant. What I said about not wanting to do the family thing was reactive, but it was also a reflection of where I'm afraid I'll fit into a family situation."

"What if a family situation came at you from out of the blue? One day you're free of it and the next day…" she shrugged "…you're a daddy, or about to become one?"

"Do you mean Lucas?"

"No, I mean…your flesh-and-blood baby."

"Can't happen. Since Nancy, there hasn't been anyone. Before her I was careful. And anyone else claiming I'm the father of their baby…" He shook his head. "Not falling for it this time. You know, fool me once…"

"And that's your final word?" she snapped.

"Deanna, what's going on here? I came to apologize for what I said, for the impression I gave you, but you're angrier than you were when I said it. So what just happened?"

"Common sense, Beau. A great big dose of common sense."

"And I'm supposed to understand that?"

"You don't have to because I finally do. Anonymous means anonymous, Beau. I should have realized that from the beginning and let it go. But now I know."

That clearly made no sense to him. Had he said something else to anger her this way? If so, he didn't know what. And even a quick rethink of his words didn't reveal anything. So now what? Chalk it up to a hormone fluctuation and let it go? Or actually consider that there were aspects to Deanna's personality that were a little off? "And you're not going to tell me?"

She laughed bitterly. "Tell you? Why would I tell you, of all people?"

"Because I thought we were friends. Even more."

Deanna drew in a steadying breath then squared her shoulders. "We are," she said. "And I'm sorry. I didn't mean..."

"Yes, you did. I don't know what that was about, or why. But you meant it, and I'm hoping it was a hormone rage." Hoping for that more than he'd hoped for anything in a long, long time.

She laid her hand across her belly protectively. "Me, too. But I know it's not. And, no, I'm not crazy, which is probably what you're thinking. I'm just coming to terms with the way I'm going to live my life, and you're in the proverbial cross-hairs as I'm working it out. It scares me. All of it scares me.

"And on top of what I already have, I've been thinking about keeping Lucas if Social Services can't find his family. I mean, I'm not even sure I can manage one child, and here I am practically on the verge of making an emotional commitment to another one. So, these questions are boiling up in me and, yes, while I may tell you I'm not crazy I'm wondering if I am. I'm also angry for things that don't make any difference to you, and it's hard to control. But that's what I'm working though right now."

"You won't let me help?"

"You can't."

He reached over and took her hand. Gave it an encouraging squeeze, which was all he meant to do. But he tried letting go, and couldn't. Her hand was a nice fit in his. It felt so natural holding it. And she wasn't resisting. Wasn't pulling away or getting restless. In fact, she seemed to be relaxing...differently. "I know how it feels being that confused. Been there a few times."

She laughed, but it was a melancholy laugh. "I think confusion is an understatement for the way I'm feeling right now. And for the way I'm going back and forth with some of the major decisions in my life."

"I hope one of those decisions is about staying here. I know I've mentioned it before, or should have if I didn't, but have you given it any serious thought?"

She went rigid and yanked her hand out of his. "I have another year on my contract, with an option to extend it a further year, with a substantial bonus. Or rather substantial penalties if I don't fulfill my obligations."

Back to square one. This was Deanna doing what Deanna did best—pulling away. His advance, her retreat. He knew better, but with her he couldn't help himself. It always slipped out.

"OK, I'm going to ask you again and hope this time you'll tell me. What's this really about?" he asked.

"I don't know what you mean."

"Yes, you do. There's something else going on. It's either about why you're really here or maybe it's about your pregnancy. I don't know, can't even venture a guess. But I know you like it here and I have an idea you've even thought about staying here and raising your baby. Yet look what you do when I mentioned that this might be a life change to consider."

"Is that how you see my staying here, as a simple life change?"

"You can stay on as my nurse, if that's what's worrying you. I've already seen how much I need help."

"Oh, right, like that's going to solve everything. I decide to stay then you decide to go."

"I haven't decided what I'm going to do."

"But it's easy for you to suggest what I should decide?"

"Deanna, please…" he cried in exasperation. "Just talk to me about it. Maybe I can help you."

"Or hurt me," she muttered. "Look, I appreciate you coming up here to explain what you meant. And I'm sorry for the way I've been acting. But…I don't know anything right now, and that's the problem. And I can't figure it out around you because…"

"Because I'm part of it?"

She nodded, brushing back tears. "Look, you've got house calls to make, and I've got a little boy to take back up to my cabin and get ready for bed. So unless you need some help with your house calls…"

"Take a walk with me, Deanna," he said, standing up. "If I can't fix what's wrong with you, at least let me try to help you relax. Help get you into a place where you can make sense of what's going on with you. Let's take that walk I offered the other night. But to a different place. A place I think you need."

She shook her head, still dazed by all the craziness coming out of her. It was like she could hear it pouring out, and she wanted to shut the dam gate but couldn't. How could she ever tell him that not only was she carrying his baby but that she'd fallen in love with him?

He might believe the love part, but he'd never believe her about the baby, which would then make her look just like Nancy to him. Someone who'd faked a baby, or a baby's paternity, just to get whatever they wanted from him.

So, no, she couldn't let herself get any closer. This wasn't a game. Wasn't some innocent flirtation, where they might spend some time together, maybe even have a brief fling. This man was the father of a baby he didn't want and didn't even know existed, and as easily as she'd told him the first part of the truth, there was no way she could be around him and not tell him the rest of it. Maybe not now, not at this very moment, but someday it would happen. That was the only thing about which she was sure.

"I, um…I'm really tired, Beau. I just want to settle in with Lucas, if you don't mind."

She glanced in the window and saw Lucas and Brax sitting on the floor, playing a game, and a lump rose in her throat. She'd made such a mess of this, starting with getting too close to Beau. Then developing feelings for him. Then, for a moment or two, actually thinking there might be a way she could settle down here, live a happy life, keep her secrets to herself.

"Half an hour. That's all I'm asking. Just thirty minutes, then you can have your evening back and I can go do my house calls."

Thirty minutes in which to dig a deeper hole. Of course, she could always crawl into it once she'd dug some more, couldn't she? "I'm not wearing hiking shoes," she argued, hoping he would just leave it alone.

But, he didn't. "You don't need hiking shoes. It's a flat walk, down to the creek." He grinned. "And I'll carry you, if I have to."

"And Lucas…"

"He's in good hands. Besides, he loves the old man. Just look at them."

She didn't have to. She'd already seen the way Lucas responded to Brax. "You're not going to give up, are you?"

"Not a chance. Even if you won't tell me about the demon you're fighting, I can still stand there to fight it with you because no one should have to tackle their demons alone."

He was just too good to be true, which made her ache all the more for what she couldn't have. But she would tell him the truth. Even with all her vacillating, she'd always known she would.

Although now she had to wait until the situation was resolved with Lucas. If she told Beau the truth *now*, the wall that would immediately go up between her and Beau could also shut out Lucas in some way. She couldn't allow that. Lucas needed the three of them united, not separated, in order to get through what he had to get through.

Funny how that worked out. She'd come here wanting to protect one baby and not sure she had the instincts to do so. But her instincts had taken on a razor-sharp precision because she was fighting to protect Lucas now as well. She didn't yet know the ending to his story, but she knew this part of it and he wasn't going to be drawn in into the mess she'd made.

Taking one more look through the window at Brax and Lucas, this was the first time she'd felt on solid ground in a while. Sad, but solid. And she was doing the right thing.

"Look, let me go and make sure Lucas is OK, then I'll be right back." Truth was, she needed a moment away from Beau to gather her wits and move forward with her plan. "Lucas," she said, stepping through the door, "Beau and I are going to go for a walk before we go back to the cabin. Is that OK with you, or would you rather go back to the cabin and get ready for bed?" Like she didn't already know the answer to that.

The boy looked up at her, clearly not happy to be interrupted in what seemed to be a very old board game—the one where you advanced your game piece until you found the lost king of candy.

Had it been Beau's game when he'd been a child? She could picture a very young Beau sprawled on the floor with his grandfather, going after that lost king in earnest. He had probably been a very serious child, much the way Lucas was. And bright. She couldn't picture him any other way. Couldn't picture Emily's baby any other way either.

"Stay here with Grandpa Brax," Lucas said. Only Brax came out more like Bwax.

"*Grandpa* Brax?" she questioned.

"He had to call me something," Brax explained, grinning a bit sheepishly.

"I suppose he did," she said, even though she knew emotions here were tugging much harder than they should. "Anyway, I'll be back in a little while. Got my phone if you need me...or Beau."

"Take your time," Brax said. "Young Mr. Lucas here is beating me royally, and I need some time to reclaim my game-board dignity"

"I'll bet," she said, then returned to the porch.

As they set off across the meadow, Deanna purposely lagged a couple of steps behind Beau, nothing obvious she hoped. Right now, close proximity was her enemy, and she wasn't walking into a battle she couldn't win.

"Is this another one of your special places?" she asked, as they approached a wooded copse.

He slowed but didn't turn to face her, so he must have sensed she didn't want to be too close to him.

"No, not really. But I thought it could be yours. It's so quiet here, it's soothing to the soul, which is what you need, Deanna. I may not understand why, and you may never tell me, but I do know it's what you need."

He was so perceptive. So caring. And this was so painful. "You're bringing me here to listen to a sound that will soothe my soul?"

"Yes. For you, and your baby." Stepping out of the meadow onto a path, he finally stopped and waited for her to catch up. Then took her by the arm. "Just so you don't trip over a tree root," he said.

"Beau, it's not that I don't want to be close to you, but with having Emily's baby and—"

"No explanations, Deanna. You don't want to be too close to me, and I accept that. But now this is for your safety. I don't want you falling."

Except she'd already fallen. And she wasn't sure she'd ever truly be able to get up again.

"Do you realize you've never once called that baby yours? It's always Emily's baby, or the baby, but not *your* baby."

"Because it is Emily's baby."

"It's your baby now, Deanna. And I don't understand what's holding you back from thinking about her or him like that. But you don't. I think you may have accepted Emily's loss but you've never let yourself accept Emily's gift. And you have to do that, Deanna. Because when you do, that's when you'll start feeling the joy you've been missing in this pregnancy. The baby is yours now. Nobody's but yours."

Glancing up to see his face, she found she couldn't because the darkness was beginning to settle in all around him. But he was so handsome even in the dimming silhouette. "I want this baby, Beau, and I want to find joy in the whole process. But sometimes life just turns into a big struggle that you can't figure out, so you simply go along and discover later on that you've gone the wrong way."

"Like I did with my wife. But I forced myself into the resolution."

"By divorcing her. I don't mean to sound trite about this, but sometimes that's the simple solution—just walk away from what doesn't work out."

"Or ignore it, which was what I did for two years. I knew exactly what I was doing but I just didn't want to go to the effort of fixing it. Then when I came here, to stay with Brax after his stroke, nothing was that good either. But after a long time of dealing with whatever I had to in order to get to the next day, I realized that one day at a time isn't enough. It doesn't make me happy because it doesn't allow me any room to hope and dream and work toward something that will make me happy.

"Which is why I asked you to help me. I'm working really hard to figure out what it is I'm going to have to do to find a life that doesn't simply exist from day to day. I think you believe that if you start thinking of Emily's baby as your baby, that gives you a life you don't think you deserve. Something more than that one-day-at-a-time existence."

There was nothing to argue because he was right. As much as it hurt, moving away from her own day-to-day existence scared her to death. Doing it without Beau scared her even more. "I don't know what I deserve," she finally said.

"But do you know what you want?"

"Pristine silence," she said. "Thirty minutes of pristine silence."

He held out his hand to her and she took it, and for the next couple of minutes as they walked along the trail neither of them spoke. At the end of the trail, save for the noise of the stream trickling over its rocky bed there was silence, and she almost believed she could clear her head here. At least, she wanted to believe it.

"Now, take off your shoes and after that you'll have a couple of options. The water is knee deep so you can roll up your pants, wade out with them down and get soaked, or take them off altogether, with the knowledge that I am a doctor and I've seen beautiful legs before."

"You've never seen my legs," she said, stepping back as his own choice was made clear. Off with his jeans.

"You've never seen mine either, but that's about to change."

He kicked off his boots, bent down and pulled off his

socks, then stood back up, unzipped then started to slide his jeans down over his hips. And while she should have turned her back, she couldn't. She wanted to imagine this was going to be something more than wading out into the creek so, like Beau, she undressed down to her panties, then took the hand he extended and waded out into the middle of the stream, where he led her to a large rock.

"This is it," he said.

"It?"

"Your thirty minutes of pristine silence. Make yourself comfortable, dangle your feet in the water if you're OK with that, and enjoy."

Then Beau sat down, and Deanna sat next to him and they both dangled their feet. And sat quietly, holding hands, for the next thirty minutes. But it was mere moments before sadness overwhelmed her again. This was where she wanted to be. With Beau. Just like this. With pristine silence in her soul.

"We're on our way," Beau said. Their thirty minutes had expired and they were halfway through a second course when reality came crashing down. "Don't let him move, even if you have to have Joey tie him to the bed."

"Really? You brought your cellphone into the pristine silence?" She thought about it for a moment, wondered where he'd tucked it, then shoved that thought completely out of her mind.

"Doctor on call," he said, sliding down off the rock and extending her his hand. "This is the escape but that's the world I live in here. No getting away from it."

She took his hand and followed him back through the water then tugged on her clothes and shoes as fast as she could. "Who is it?"

"Arthur. Brax and Joey and Lucas are up at his house. It's a heart attack."

"No," she whispered, as they set off down the trail. "How far out are we?"

"Twenty minutes, if we hurry. But I don't want you running. Not out here, in the dark."

"Then go on without me. You get to him as fast as you can and I'll go to the clinic to get things set to receive him. I'm assuming we'll transport him somewhere else but we can get the preliminaries taken care of at the clinic first."

"We'll transport him if he's stable enough. And if he lets us. Arthur isn't always...co-operative."

"You just go take care of him, OK?"

"I don't like leaving you out here."

"I'm a big girl, Beau. If I can take care of myself in New York, I sure as heck can do it here. So, please..."

"Stay on the trail. And call me if—"

"No ifs. Just go. *Please*. Take care of him!"

He turned away from her but didn't move. Instead, he turned back around to face her, took two giant steps forward, pulled her into his arms and kissed her. It was a short kiss but powerful. A kiss she wanted, at another time, another place. Where there was less confusion. But she didn't have any time for that as she was still reeling from the shock of it, trying to make sense of it, when Beau pulled back and let out a deep breath.

"The first kiss was to see if there would be a second one. The second one gives us something to talk about," he said, then didn't wait for Deanna to respond. Rather, he bypassed the laid-out trail and went crashing through the trees and undergrowth in a direction she didn't know. But she heard him for several seconds, and felt him for even longer than that.

When the full realization of what had just happened

sank in, she laid her hand on her belly and sighed. "Your daddy just kissed me again," she said. Then smiled. "And I liked it. So now let's you and me talk some things out on the way back to the clinic, and see if we can figure out where to go from here. Because it won't work. And my heart is breaking. And I want you to get to know him. And I'm so…scared."

CHAPTER TEN

BIG MAN BROUGHT down by an arrhythmia. As Deanna inserted an IV into Arthur Handler's arm, she realized that she couldn't go back to research and organization. Not on a full-time basis. What she did was important because it made medical services in areas like this possible, but after being part of those medical services and making a different kind of difference, her world had to be about both, and she was going to have to figure out a way to make that work. That, among so many other things.

"You're going to feel a stick," she said, noticing the man was looking away, squeezing his eyes shut as tightly as he could.

"Don't need an IV," he grumbled.

"Maybe you wouldn't have if you'd mentioned to any of us that you've been getting these chest twinges for a few weeks. But you didn't. So now it's an IV..." She poked it into his arm carefully then taped it in place.

"You're not very sympathetic," he snapped. "Good thing you do research and not patient care, because there's not a sane doctor in the country who'd have you as his nurse."

Words spoken in fear. Deanna knew that and didn't take them personally. In fact, her reaction was to take hold of Arthur's hand and simply hold it. "You're going to be fine, Arthur. I doubt you'll be in the hospital more than a couple of days, and after that you'll be recuperating…" He couldn't go home, because it was too isolated, and there was no way he should be alone. "Recuperating in the cabin, with your least favorite nurse taking care of you for a while."

Yet another commitment to keep her here a while longer. It was amazing how her life was expanding in so many directions, and all of it felt so right and so wrong at the same time.

"Will you stick needles in me then?" He tried to grumble, but the best he could muster was something that sounded more like a scratchy throat.

"Probably," she teased. "Because I'm very good at it. Rather enjoy torturing people like you."

In response he squeezed her hand but still refused to look at her. "So, who's flying me?"

"Joey's the pilot, and Beau and I thought we'd hop a ride in just to annoy you." Adjusting the IV bag to a slow drip, she didn't attach any medication to it as Beau had already given Arthur a nitroglycerine pill, which had relieved his symptoms almost immediately. The IV was precautionary, in the event they had to get other meds in fast.

"You shouldn't go," Arthur said.

"Because I'm pregnant?"

"Too much stress. You should stay here and rest."

"I'm going to have some tests run in the morning so whether it's now or then, I've got to take a ride." It was time to move forward differently with her life. She wasn't sure yet what that meant, but getting the proper tests, especially with her better than average chance of a multiple birth, was the first step.

"And the ride's ready," Beau said, coming up behind her and slipping an arm around her waist. "Brax will be fine with Lucas, so we're good to go."

Good to go. Airplanes were fine, but helicopters… Deanna drew in a deep breath and braced herself. The ride was going to be bumpy in more ways than one.

OK, maybe the kiss hadn't been the best idea he'd ever had but, damn it, how could he *not* have kissed her? Sure, there were complications. Her emotions, the fact she wouldn't let him in. And if she went back to New York…well, he could go back there with her. His job was certainly still open. And maybe that's what he'd do, even after all the fuss of trying to figure out how to make his life work here. The truth of the matter was it would work perfectly right here in Sugar Creek, Tennessee, if Deanna stayed. So far, she didn't seem inclined to.

"You comfortable?" he asked her. She was strapped into one of the two passenger seats across from him, while he was in the jump seat next to the stretcher.

"Not sure. I've never been in a helicopter before, so I don't know what comfortable's supposed to feel like. But I'm OK."

"You look…"

"Worried? I am. Not about the flight. But I've decided to go through with the tests tomorrow, since we'll be at the hospital anyway. And I've been thinking, what if…?"

Beau shook his head and reached across Arthur to take hold of Deanna's hand. "No what-ifs, OK? Everything is going to be fine."

"But it could be twins, or more."

"Or it could be one, perfectly healthy, beautiful baby. Although twins are good."

Deanna leaned back in her seat, shut her eyes and moaned. Out loud.

"Motion sickness?" Beau asked, as Deanna's hand slipped out of his.

She shook her head but didn't say a word. So Beau chalked it up to flight jitters and didn't bother her. Just let her sit there, looking a bit miserable. Until...

Her eyes shot open. A pain was ripping through her side. Hot knife. Searing. Fast. Complete. Then gone.

"What?" he asked.

She didn't know what. It had come and gone in a second. "Nothing. Just not liking the ride so much." Probably a touch of indigestion. Yes, that's what it was. Indigestion, foe of many a mom-to-be.

"That wasn't a 'nothing' expression on your face, Deanna."

"It was a totally 'nothing' expression," Deanna said defensively, clamping her arm against her side to splint herself in case the pain hit again.

"She's a very self-sacrificing young lady, Beau. If she was in pain, I don't believe she'd tell you," Arthur interjected.

"I *said* I'm fine," she snapped.

"There's my proof, Beau. Deanna's being snappy. Better take heed."

"OK, indigestion," Deanna admitted. "I don't always eat the way I should." Another shooting pain hit her, only this time it went from her lower right abdomen and wrapped round to her back. Beau was immediately at her side. He stepped over Arthur and planted himself in the seat next to Deanna.

"Describe the pain."

She nodded. "Sharp, intermittent." She showed him where. "And it just started. I'm not like Arthur..." she glanced down at the man, and forced a smile "...who had *twinges* for weeks."

After a quick assessment of Deanna's vital signs, Beau prodded her lower right abdomen, which elicited a moan.

"You've had those back spasms. And you were nauseated earlier," he said. "Was it morning sickness or something else?"

"I haven't had morning sickness, and this far along I was surprised it would start. So maybe it wasn't…" A pain grabbed her so hard she gasped. "It's risky, having my appendix out while I'm pregnant, but I think…"

He took hold of her left hand. "Not as risky as you'd think. Medical technology has come a long way in protecting both mother and baby during something like this. The bigger risk is not having it fixed, and taking a chance at a rupture."

"Am I in trouble?" she asked him. "I didn't know anything was wrong."

"If it's appendicitis, the longer you wait the more likely it is you'll have complications. As the uterus gets bigger, it basically pushes the appendix up towards the right kidney. That causes the pain you'd expect with appendicitis, but because of the shifting around going on, back pain is common. Which you've been having. Also, appendicitis can mimic other things, like a kidney infection. Then there would be the typical symptoms of appendicitis—nausea, vomiting, loss of appetite, which you've been experiencing as well."

"So, I've been having appendicitis for a while. And I've put my baby at risk?"

"It's early, Deanna. Everything's going to be fine."

"And in my defense," Arthur said from his stretcher, "there was nothing differentiating my twinges from the indigestion I suffer after eating a fine French meal. *Foie gras…*" He raised his hand to his mouth and kissed his fingertips, even though they were impeded by his oxygen mask. "Food of the gods."

"And food of your past," Beau said.

"The indignities we must endure," the old man said, then reached up and took hold of Deanna's right hand. "After we land, I'm sure we'll be parted, Deanna. But I want you to know that after your surgery I'd be delighted to spend my convalescence with you convalescing at my side. Helping each other as we are able to. And your surgery will go splendidly, my dear. Simply splendidly. For both you and the unborn Lambert."

She hoped so. Shutting her eyes and leaning her head against the helicopter's cabin wall, she discovered she was too numb to think. The pain didn't matter. It came and went, and as soon as they operated, it would be gone permanently. But she was so frightened for the baby. It was an indescribable feeling…something that came from a place she didn't fully understand.

Part of the feeling was the possibility of losing Emily altogether. She knew that. But there was something else…the possibility of her own loss. She wanted this baby. Not just for Emily. She wanted it for herself because…because she loved it. Truly loved it. Because it was her baby. Her baby.

"My baby," she whispered, as tears slid from behind her closed eyes. "It's my baby."

"Arthur's squared away in Cardiac Care, and mad as hell because he can't be down here to support you," Beau said.

He looked so good in surgical scrubs. Even through the pain and the first round of IV drugs, that's the first thing she thought when Beau entered the ER room. So handsome. "How long before I go in?"

"About ten minutes."

"Are you going to be in there?"

"I can't," he whispered, pulling a chrome stool up to the side of her bed and sitting down. "They'll let me observe from the window but I'm too…involved to scrub in."

"I wish you could," she said, reaching through the rungs of the bed rails to take hold of his hand. It was time. She knew it. Everything inside her knew it was finally time. Because his baby was at risk, and he did have the right to know. His baby, her baby... "Am I approved for the laparoscopic procedure?"

That meant the surgeon would make several tiny cuts in her abdomen and insert a miniature camera and surgical instruments, then watch the image of the procedure on the screen as he removed the appendix. Totally unlike traditional surgery with general anesthesia, a large incision and direct observation of the appendix, this was less invasive, required less anesthesia and recovery time was much faster.

"The obstetrics team thinks you're a good candidate. Your uterus hasn't expanded so much that your appendix won't be seen through the camera, and you're in good health. So it's a go, and they're scrubbing in too, just to be there."

"Good hands," she murmured.

"Very good hands. It's an excellent hospital."

"I mean yours," she said, as she fought back the preanesthetic grogginess overtaking her.

"Look, Deanna. Before they take you, there's something I want you to know. About that kiss..."

"You didn't like it?" she interrupted.

"No. I loved it. It wasn't a mistake. Neither time."

"Could have been longer," she said. Her words were slurring now. She could hear them and they came out with such effort... *Have to tell him. Now. He has to know.*

"It will be longer next time," he said. "If that's what you want. I've done a lot of thinking, but now's not the time to talk about this. So..."

"Shh," she said, raising her finger to her lips to silence him and totally missing her face. "I have to talk now."

He chuckled. "You won't be talking for long."

"Which is why I have to say this now. The baby—"

"Will be fine," he interrupted. "I know that's your biggest fear. But the baby will be fine."

"My baby," she said, fighting to stay awake.

"Of course it's your baby." He lowered his face to her hand and kissed the back of it. "And you're going to be the best mother—"

"Your baby," she said.

"Yes, I'll love it like it's my baby."

"It *is* your baby," she said, as her eyes started to flutter shut. "Emily's egg, your sperm. Your baby…"

"No way."

"Your baby," she said one final time, then drifted off.

"How's she doing?" Brax asked. He was strolling down the hall like he belonged there. No cane, no limp. A totally revitalized man.

Beau nodded. "They just took her in. I'm going to go…" He looked at his grandfather. "Where's Lucas?"

"With Kelli Dawson. She's looking after him for the day."

"She said something, Brax. Deanna said something I don't understand, and maybe it's because she was most of the way under, but…" He thought about her words again. Put together, they made sense. But in the whole context of his life they didn't.

"Judging from they way you're as white as a ghost, I'd say whatever she told you was pretty earth-shaking."

"To put it mildly. She told me the baby she's carrying is mine. To cut a long story short, she was carrying her cousin's baby, and her cousin died. Deanna said her cousin's egg was impregnated with my sperm. Earlier she told me that the reason her cousin's husband didn't want the baby was that the insemination had been done with the wrong sperm. But—"

"Maybe it's true. Mistakes happen..." Brax shrugged. "Or maybe what she said was simply the anesthetic ramblings of a woman in love who wants the man she loves to be the father of her baby. That's been known to happen, too."

"She loves me?"

"Are you blind, son? That woman turned her life upside down, and it wasn't because she's clamoring for a future here in Sugar Creek. She's been clamoring for you. You're in love with her, aren't you?"

"Maybe I am."

"Maybe, my ass." Brax squared his shoulders. "Deanna Lambert's the finest woman you're ever going to have in your life. If you let her into your life. And if you want my opinion—"

"Like I could stop you," Beau interrupted.

Not to be dissuaded, Brax continued, "If you want my opinion, you'd be a damned fool to let her get away. Unless it's her baby that's stopping you. Is that why you're out here with me rather than barging your way into surgery and letting her know you're with her every step of the way?"

Was it the baby that was causing him to hesitate? Or his fear that when she was better she'd go back to being the Deanna Lambert who wanted to go it alone? "I don't know," he admitted.

"Then I'd suggest you find out, son. Instead of complicating the thing, simplify it. If you love her, tell her, then find a way to make it work."

"Easy for you to say," Beau said, then he headed down

the surgical hall and straight into the scrub room. The thing was, it was easy for him to say, too.

"I love Deanna Lambert," he said, as he tapped the faucet on with his foot and began the scrubbing routine. "I love Deanna Lambert." So now it was time to step up to that love and find out if she loved him back. Or be miserable in silence for a long, long time. Maybe for ever.

Oh, how she didn't want to wake up, but that's what the voices were telling her to do. Cloudy voices, distant voices. And…she could hear Beau.

"Wake up, Deanna. It's over now. Baby's doing fine, and you're doing fine."

Baby's doing fine. Beautiful words that made her feel so much better. "Your baby," she murmured.

"We'll talk about that later. Right now, you just need to concentrate on opening your eyes."

Other voices she didn't recognize chimed in. They wanted her eyes open, too. "Don't want to," she shouted, or was she just whispering? In her head it all sounded the same.

"Sure you do. You want to wake up and open your eyes."

Beau's voice again. For him, she did want to wake up and open her eyes. Only for him. "Love him," she murmured. "I love him."

"I think that was meant for you," Brax said.

Brax, what was he doing here? He shouldn't be here, too. "Lucas?" she forced herself to say.

"He's fine. Don't worry. Kelli Dawson is keeping him until one of us gets back to Sugar Creek." Beau brushed his fingers across her cheek. "And if you ever even hint that you don't have maternal instincts, Deanna Lambert, I'm going remind you of your first two concerns coming out of anesthesia. "

"But he's OK," she said, sighing. "That's good, because I'm going to keep him if I can." Now she felt better. Lucas was fine. Her baby was fine. Beau was here. "All good," she said, then let the clouds roll over her consciousness for a while longer.

"It's about time," Beau said, only a moment later.

This time she did open her eyes, and the only person she saw was Beau. "How long was I...?"

"We tried waking you a couple of hours ago, but you weren't ready. Once you knew that Lucas and your baby were fine, you drifted off with a smile on your face. A beautiful smile."

"Hope I didn't say anything I shouldn't."

"Nothing you shouldn't, but..." He paused then walked over to the window. It was a small hospital in a beautiful area, and Deanna's view for the next couple of days would be a mountain. "But some of the things you were trying to tell me were...well, pretty crazy. About the baby being..."

"Yours?"

"It's not an easy subject for me, Deanna." He turned to face her. "I know you were in a lot of pain then under anesthesia, so I understand that some of the things you said might be a little off. But there's something you have to know. Back when I was married, my wife drove me crazy with her obsession with getting pregnant. Every day, every night she came at me with it and I gave in to something I shouldn't have done.

"Like I told you, she'd come to the hospital, and it was embarrassing me. She asked me to bank my sperm so if I wasn't available when she was ovulating... I did, because I was feeling so guilty and so pressured. Then when you told me the baby you're carrying is mine, and you said there was a mix-up with the sperm used in fertilizing Emily's egg..."

He drew in a ragged breath. "To cut a long story short, I found an e-mail from Nancy to her lawyer, asking him approximately how much she'd be entitled to if she had my baby as opposed to how much she'd get if she simply walked away.

"I'd had this inheritance from my mother and she wanted as much as she could get. So I had the sperm destroyed, gave her a settlement just to be done with it, and... and that's about it. Until you said..."

"I'm having your baby. I'm so sorry, but it's the truth. My cousin Emily—her husband's name is Alexander Braxton and it seems *his* sperm was destroyed accidentally. Maybe in place of yours, I don't know. But Emily's egg was fertilized with your sperm. My lawyers had to fight to get the information, but that's what happened.

"And when Emily found out, she told Alex, who said he wasn't going to raise another man's child. He gave Emily a choice—him or her baby. She chose her baby, and she was leaving him when..." She shut her eyes. "It was raining that night, she missed a turn. And I became a real mother to her child. My child. Your child. Except with the things you've said..."

"Damn," he muttered.

"You have a right to question me, Beau. I understand. Especially after what Nancy—"

"No. I don't question what you're saying, Deanna. You're not lying to me. But that's what your conflicts have been about, isn't it? Telling me."

"I tried, Beau. So many times I tried. But I was scared, because I was falling in love with you and I didn't know..."

"You didn't know what I would do because of all the stupid things I said. Deanna, I'm so sorry. You were hearing my anger, because I've never completely put it behind me. Brax keeps telling me I need to move on, but it's like so many things in my life were frozen in place. Until I met you. Then I wanted that change to happen, but you never let me in completely, so, instead of risking being hurt again, I put up my defenses. And I'm so sorry."

"But you didn't know. How could you? I'm the one who should be apologizing because I never meant to hurt you, Beau."

"Would you have told me if the baby's life hadn't been in danger?"

"I would have. But I thought that would put up a wall between us that would never come down, and because Lucas and Brax... I really do want to adopt Lucas if I can, so I had to consider what was best for him, and that was being around you and Brax. He needs you both right now, and I didn't want my situation to pull him away from you. After his situation was resolved, I would have told you about the baby. I promise, I would have told you."

"And now I'm going to be a father," he said somberly.

"Any way you want to do it, Beau. You do have a choice in this, and I'll respect it."

"Did you come to Sugar Creek to spy on me?" he asked, a twinkle popping into his eyes.

"Spying was all I meant to do. I knew what kind of person Emily was, but I wanted to know what kind of person my baby's father was. I think it was part of my need to put off accepting how my life was changing, the real pain of missing my cousin, maybe a whole lot of other things I haven't figured out yet. But I wanted to know, wanted to see for myself."

"Then look what happened."

"Just look," she murmured, as her eyelids started to flutter down.

"Before you go back to sleep, would you answer one more question for me?" he asked, leaning over the bed rail.

"I'll try," she said, her eyes not opening again.

"Will you marry me, Deanna? Stay here in Sugar Creek with me? Raise our baby together, adopt Lucas, put up with my hectic lifestyle and deal with my cantankerous old grandfather? Or do it in New York and start a new life together there. Any way you want to do it, because I love you."

"With you," she said. "I want to do it with…" Sigh. Over and out.

"Well, it wasn't the most romantic proposal, but I'll do it again, Deanna. When you'll remember it." He bent over and kissed her on the forehead, then pulled aside her gown, looked at her belly, bandaged as it was, and smiled. "Our baby."

"Emily Rose Alexander," Deanna said, cradling her daughter in her arms. "Do you know how much your mommy and daddy love you?" They were living in the ranch house now, and Brax had bought and moved to the cabin up on the ridge, happy to be someplace with a better view. He was practicing medicine again in a limited capacity, mornings only, while Beau and Lucas tended the horses. And Deanna was continuing her consultant work, but only part time, and always with her daughter close by.

In their efforts to expand medical services, Beau and Deanna had even brought in a pediatrician to take care of the increasing kiddie population in the area. The clinic was expanding, life was expanding, and it was everything Emily would have wanted for her daughter. Everything Deanna wanted for *her* daughter and son.

"When can she come outside and play with me?" Lucas asked impatiently. The same question he'd been asking for weeks.

"Not for a few years," Beau said, settling down on the

couch next to Deanna. "And, Lucas, you'd better put on your boots because your grandpa is on his way here to give you a riding lesson."

"Grandpa's more fun than Emily," Lucas said. "She can't do anything."

Beau and Deanna looked at each other, smiling. Lucas was legally their son now. There hadn't been much of a legal ordeal since there was no family to be found. And he was turning into a grandpa's boy. Great-grandpa, actually. Of course Brax was spoiling him rotten. "And Grandpa's going to teach Emily to ride when she's old enough," Beau said.

As Lucas scampered off in pursuit of his riding boots, Deanna handed Emily over to Beau then started to stand up. But he grabbed her hand and pulled her back down to the sofa next to him.

"As much as I'd love staying here with the two of you, I've got a couple of patients coming in this afternoon."

"But I'm the doctor," Beau said, as he made faces at his daughter.

"And I'm the nurse who shares her husband's practice, and handles minor cases so he can have more time with his family." She smiled. "Remember the plan to keep you less obsessed?"

"I've got a house call later on. And I promised Arthur I'd stop by for a few minutes. He's writing a book on his journey from heart attack to fitness guru and he wants me to check a couple of his medical facts."

"And I've got to take Lucas for pizza while you're gone. It's a date for just the two of us, and Brax is going to have an evening alone with Emily, which he's been pestering me about for days."

"What about us?" Beau said, feigning a hurt expression. "When do we get some time alone?"

"Trust me, I've got you penciled in. Tonight. Champagne. Dim lights. Soft music. Hot tub for starters."

"Then what?" he asked, his attention now fully diverted from Emily to Deanna.

"Everything," Deanna said, scooting in closer to him, then laying her head on his shoulder. "Absolutely everything."

* * * * *

Mills & Boon® Hardback

May 2013

ROMANCE

A Rich Man's Whim	Lynne Graham
A Price Worth Paying?	Trish Morey
A Touch of Notoriety	Carole Mortimer
The Secret Casella Baby	Cathy Williams
Maid for Montero	Kim Lawrence
Captive in his Castle	Chantelle Shaw
Heir to a Dark Inheritance	Maisey Yates
A Legacy of Secrets	Carol Marinelli
Her Deal with the Devil	Nicola Marsh
One More Sleepless Night	Lucy King
A Father for Her Triplets	Susan Meier
The Matchmaker's Happy Ending	Shirley Jump
Second Chance with the Rebel	Cara Colter
First Comes Baby...	Michelle Douglas
Anything but Vanilla...	Liz Fielding
It was Only a Kiss	Joss Wood
Return of the Rebel Doctor	Joanna Neil
One Baby Step at a Time	Meredith Webber

MEDICAL

NYC Angels: Flirting with Danger	Tina Beckett
NYC Angels: Tempting Nurse Scarlet	Wendy S. Marcus
One Life Changing Moment	Lucy Clark
P.S. You're a Daddy!	Dianne Drake

0413 GEN STD HB

Mills & Boon® Large Print
May 2013

ROMANCE

Beholden to the Throne	Carol Marinelli
The Petrelli Heir	Kim Lawrence
Her Little White Lie	Maisey Yates
Her Shameful Secret	Susanna Carr
The Incorrigible Playboy	Emma Darcy
No Longer Forbidden?	Dani Collins
The Enigmatic Greek	Catherine George
The Heir's Proposal	Raye Morgan
The Soldier's Sweetheart	Soraya Lane
The Billionaire's Fair Lady	Barbara Wallace
A Bride for the Maverick Millionaire	Marion Lennox

HISTORICAL

Some Like to Shock	Carole Mortimer
Forbidden Jewel of India	Louise Allen
The Caged Countess	Joanna Fulford
Captive of the Border Lord	Blythe Gifford
Behind the Rake's Wicked Wager	Sarah Mallory

MEDICAL

Maybe This Christmas…?	Alison Roberts
A Doctor, A Fling & A Wedding Ring	Fiona McArthur
Dr Chandler's Sleeping Beauty	Melanie Milburne
Her Christmas Eve Diamond	Scarlet Wilson
Newborn Baby For Christmas	Fiona Lowe
The War Hero's Locked-Away Heart	Louisa George

0413 GEN STD LP

ROMANCE

The Sheikh's Prize	Lynne Graham
Forgiven but not Forgotten?	Abby Green
His Final Bargain	Melanie Milburne
A Throne for the Taking	Kate Walker
Diamond in the Desert	Susan Stephens
A Greek Escape	Elizabeth Power
Princess in the Iron Mask	Victoria Parker
An Invitation to Sin	Sarah Morgan
Too Close for Comfort	Heidi Rice
The Right Mr Wrong	Natalie Anderson
The Making of a Princess	Teresa Carpenter
Marriage for Her Baby	Raye Morgan
The Man Behind the Pinstripes	Melissa McClone
Falling for the Rebel Falcon	Lucy Gordon
Secrets & Saris	Shoma Narayanan
The First Crush Is the Deepest	Nina Harrington
One Night She Would Never Forget	Amy Andrews
When the Cameras Stop Rolling...	Connie Cox

MEDICAL

NYC Angels: Making the Surgeon Smile	Lynne Marshall
NYC Angels: An Explosive Reunion	Alison Roberts
The Secret in His Heart	Caroline Anderson
The ER's Newest Dad	Janice Lynn

0513 GEN STD HB

Mills & Boon® Large Print
June 2013

ROMANCE

Sold to the Enemy	Sarah Morgan
Uncovering the Silveri Secret	Melanie Milburne
Bartering Her Innocence	Trish Morey
Dealing Her Final Card	Jennie Lucas
In the Heat of the Spotlight	Kate Hewitt
No More Sweet Surrender	Caitlin Crews
Pride After Her Fall	Lucy Ellis
Her Rocky Mountain Protector	Patricia Thayer
The Billionaire's Baby SOS	Susan Meier
Baby out of the Blue	Rebecca Winters
Ballroom to Bride and Groom	Kate Hardy

HISTORICAL

Never Trust a Rake	Annie Burrows
Dicing with the Dangerous Lord	Margaret McPhee
Haunted by the Earl's Touch	Ann Lethbridge
The Last de Burgh	Deborah Simmons
A Daring Liaison	Gail Ranstrom

MEDICAL

From Christmas to Eternity	Caroline Anderson
Her Little Spanish Secret	Laura Iding
Christmas with Dr Delicious	Sue MacKay
One Night That Changed Everything	Tina Beckett
Christmas Where She Belongs	Meredith Webber
His Bride in Paradise	Joanna Neil

0513 GEN STD LP